ABOUT THE AUTHOR

Maggie Anderson is an Australian writer of romance, urban fantasy, supernatural crime thrillers and YA thrillers. She is currently working on a fourth romance novel, yet to be titled, as well as the third book in her Dark Legacy series, *Soul Chaser*. Maggie resides in Brisbane, Queensland. You can find out more about her books at: www.m-anderson.com.au

Books by Maggie Anderson

Driving Me Crazy
Love's Twist of Fate
A Night of Passion
A Night of Passion CRE
Christmas, Mistletoe and You

Paranormal Romance Series

Wolf Blood
Wolf Curse
Wolf Lover (2019)

Urban Fantasy Series
Writing as M. A. Anderson

REECE: Prequel
Dark Legacy
Once Bitten
Soul Chaser
Evil Nature

A
Night Of
Passion

Clean Romance Edition

MAGGIE ANDERSON

Bella Luna Books
Australia

Revised edition 2019

Front and back cover photos from
canstockphoto.com

Cover design by Maggie Anderson
Brisbane, Australia

ISBN-13:9780992513955

Published by Bella Luna Books
AUSTRALIA

To romance readers everywhere. Enjoy!

Prologue

Prue had been sitting at the bar in Hemingway's Cafe during Happy Hour, contemplating whether to leave or stay when he appeared on the stool beside her and offered to buy her a cocktail. She didn't usually accept drinks from strange men but tonight would be different. She needed him, needed to feel desired again, needed to be touched in a way she hadn't been in a long time, even if it was only for the briefest moment. He didn't give his name nor did he ask for hers, which was fine with her, and after an hour of idle chit chat they ended up in a luxury hotel suite not far from the bar. At least it wasn't a dive of a motel that would make the experience seem cheap and dirty, and for that she was grateful. She had never done anything like it before—it wasn't in her nature to pick up men—nor would she do it again.

They had walked the couple of blocks to the hotel in the warm, summer evening air hand in hand, chatting and laughing—although both nervous—like they had known each other for years. Prue was pleased that *this* man had offered to buy her a drink. She knew tonight would be everything she hoped for.

After a couple of hours making sweet passionate love to each other, he gazed into her eyes and his gentle fingers brushed her long blonde hair from her flushed cheeks. She was beautiful. Lying beside her, he pulled Prue into his arms and kissed her forehead. "I hope it was good for you."

"It was." She glanced up into his attractive face and gave a shy smile. "You?"

His smile broadened. "Yes, it was." He kissed her forehead again. "Very good."

Prue felt comfortable in his arms. It had been three years since she'd been in a relationship and wondered what it would be like to be with this man. Get to know him. But as they had already agreed it was to be only one night, what hope did she have? She hadn't given any thought to the possibility that he could be married.

Something she didn't want to think about.

As the thought crossed her mind, he eased her out of his arms and headed to the bathroom. "Won't be long."

She heard the shower run and after several minutes he returned wearing a white hotel towel wrapped around his waist. Her eyes followed his lithe muscular frame across the room, and she wished he was hers. He seemed decent, and had been more than attentive during their lovemaking. Not once had she felt like a one night stand. He'd made her feel desired.

He gazed at her lying naked in the bed and smiled. "Can I drop you somewhere?" he asked, zipping his pants and shrugging into his white business shirt.

Prue's thoughts were pulled back to reality. This was all there would be. They had satisfied their needs and now it was goodbye. "Thanks, but I don't have far to go."

He stared at her for several seconds as though he wanted to say something, but then turned around and continued dressing. Within minutes he was ready to leave. He moved across the room to the king-sized bed, leaned in and kissed her on the lips. "It's been a pleasure. Take care of yourself."

Prue smiled up at him, tears stinging the backs of her eyes. She wouldn't cry. She knew what tonight had been, even though now she wished she hadn't agreed to it. "Yes, it has. You too."

He picked up his jacket from off the chair and headed to the door. Before leaving he turned around, studied Prue once more, then opened the door and walked out of her life.

One

Prue Granger stepped into the busy corner deli opposite the broadcast center to pick up a vanilla latte before facing her first day on the job. She had landed the role of personal assistant to Rachelle Reed, one of New York's top morning talk show hosts, and had recently moved to The Big Apple from Pittsburgh. It was a culture shock, to say the least, but the city had already found a place in her heart.

She had been in a lessor role at WTAE Channel 4, for the past five years, attempting to work her way up the media corporate ladder to become a production manager on their regular morning show, but when the job had been handed to an outsider, Prue knew it was time to look further afield. She was nervous and excited about working with Rachelle as she walked along the sidewalk carrying the container of hot coffee. It was a chilly winter morning and the city was bustling with pedestrians, taxis, cars and couriers making their way to wherever they had to be for the day.

Prue knew this move was a huge opportunity for her and she was going to do everything she could to ensure her success. It was a dream come true. She had been told that a thousand other girls would have killed for the opportunity to work with Rachelle, and Prue realized she would have to step up her game if she wanted to retain the position and move up in the world of television.

She approached the front entrance and gazed up at the large black CBS Broadcast Center sign emblazoned on the side of the stainless steel marquee and sighed. She was here at last and about to start a new phase in her life. One she hoped would take her career to a whole new level.

When she walked over to the revolving door, the glass one beside it swung open and a young man held it for her to step through.

Prue smiled. "Thanks. You're a gentleman."

"My pleasure." He held out his hand. "I'm Gabe Hamilton, welcome to CBS. We'll be working together on Rachelle's show."

How did he know who she was? She shook his hand. "I'm Prue Granger, but you already knew that, didn't you?"

"Yes... and I'm not psychic." His smile broadened and he raised his left hand. It contained a blue manila folder with her name on it.

"Oh, of course," she said, her smile widening.

"Ok, follow me." He led her along the ground floor corridor lined with lightboxes of current News and TV presenters. "These smiling faces are our news, current affairs and talk show hosts. You'll see them floating around the building from time to time." He headed back along the corridor. "The elevator's this way. Before we get started, you should be aware that Rachelle can be a bit of a diva at times, but you'll get used to it. She's a nice enough person until you make a mistake and end up on her wrong side. I guess you could say she's passionate about her job."

Prue's stomach did an uneasy flip flop. "I thought she was meant to be lovely. That's what I've been told."

"Don't get me wrong, she is lovely, but she can be dramatic sometimes. When that happens all hell breaks loose. She is, after all, one of the *top* talk show hosts in New York, in the US for that matter. Goes with the territory."

Prue was grateful for the heads up. She wanted to make a good impression on the CBS hierarchy and Rachelle Reed. She planned to move up the ladder this time and not be knocked back for someone younger with less experience. "Good to know. Thanks."

"No problem."

The elevator doors swished open and Prue and Gabe stepped inside. "I'll show you around and introduce you to the people you'll be working with. Always a good icebreaker before your first show."

"Thanks, I really appreciate it." Prue's heart did a little shudder. Joining a new team and being the new kid on the block was difficult at best, there was bound to be someone who didn't like her, but she was determined to make it work.

"We usually record two shows with the same audience and do a seat swap during the break. It's fairly painless. You'll need to be here bright and early tomorrow morning for the briefing before the show."

"Oh, ok, what time?" She glanced at her watch although she didn't know why.

"Seven thirty."

Prue wanted to show him she was a flexible team player. "Sure, no problem. I can be here."

"Great." The elevator stopped and the doors slid open. "Here we are." He gestured for her to step out. "After you."

"Thanks." She stepped into the corridor, Gabe following her.

"Ok, let's get started."

After doing the rounds and introductions, Gabe escorted Prue to Rachelle's dressing room. He knocked.

"Go away." Came the warning from inside.

"Rachelle, I have Prue Granger with me, your new personal assistant. She would very much like to meet you." He gave Prue an uncertain smile and mouthed, "This is what I mean."

The door flew open. "Well why didn't you say so?" She threw out her hand. "Hi. Nice to meet you."

Prue reached for Rachelle's hand but the TV host turned and strutted back to the mirror to check her makeup.

Gabe cleared his throat and motioned for Prue to go in. Prue wasn't sure she should. She shook her head. "After you," Gabe said, motioning with his head.

Prue decided to try some reverse psychology. "I can see Rachelle is busy so we can make it another time."

Rachelle swung around, pursed her lips and gave Prue the once over. "No, it's fine. Come on in. Better now than never."

Prue gave Gabe an unsure glance before stepping through the doorway and wondered what she had gotten herself into.

$\mathcal{T}$wo

After six months in the role, Prue had become an integral member of The Rachelle Reed Show and felt as though she had always worked there. She loved the friendly atmosphere, it was more like a family environment than a workplace, and she'd made some great friends too. She had also managed to form a best friendship with Rachelle. Go figure. They had become so close they told each other everything. And as it turned out, Rachelle was a nice person who was, as Gabe had said, passionate about giving her viewers a quality show and candid interviews with extraordinary people.

This morning was no different. Rachelle would be interviewing Nicholas Colton, one of New York Times and USA Today's bestselling thriller authors. He had written fifteen successful novels over the past six years and had shot to celebrity status with his debut title, *The Contract Killer*. Rachelle was in a whirl over having the esteemed, award-winning author on her show. And he was male model attractive too.

Prue had been instructed to meet and greet Mr. Colton and to escort him to the green room. She had no idea what he looked like, as in her haste to get down to reception she'd forgotten to collect the author's profile from Rachelle's office and didn't have time to go back for it. She'd just have to keep her wits about her and scrutinize every good-looking male that came through the revolving door. That could be fun. When she reached the foyer, Prue noticed an entourage of fans waiting outside the building, books in hand, hoping to get an autograph when the author arrived.

He'd only have ten minutes, and that would be cutting it fine. But, of course, he couldn't disappoint readers, they were his livelihood and the station knew that.

Prue was curious. She slipped through one of the glass side doors and wandered over to a middle-aged woman standing on the sidewalk to ask about the author.

"Oh, he's wonderful. I love his books. I have 'em all, you know," the woman gushed. "And he's so handsome to boot." She passed the novel in her hand to Prue and turned it over to show her the back cover photo. "I'm so glad to be here for the show. I missed his latest book signing."

When Prue saw the photo her face paled and the woman asked if she was alright. Prue looked at her dazed. "Huh? Yes, I'm fine. I have to go. Thank you." She shoved the book at the woman, disappeared through the revolving door and headed for her friend's dressing room.

Rachelle had finished having her hair and makeup done and was slipping into a designer, navy blue dress when the door flew open and Prue barged in. "Whatever happened to knocking, hon?"

"It's him." Prue blurted. Her face flushed, her breathing ragged.

Rachelle dashed over to her and sat her on a chair. "Take it easy, honey. Who?"

"Nicholas Colton."

The TV host glanced through the open doorway. "He's here already?" She was keen to meet the man in person. Maybe they could have a drink later.

Prue shook her head. "Not yet."

Rachelle frowned and sat down beside her. "Then what's all the excitement about?"

Prue's heart was racing. She could barely breathe. "It's him."

"You said that already, honey. What do you mean?"

"He's the one night stand I told you about."

Rachelle's eyes widened. "Nicholas Colton? Oh, good lord, are you sure? What are you going to do?"

Prue popped up off the chair. "Yes, I'm one hundred percent sure. Gabe can meet him when he arrives. I can't do it, he'll recognize me."

"Maybe he won't. It's been five years. And besides, what man remembers a one night stand?"

Prue gave her an irritated frown. She hoped she wouldn't have been that easy to forget. "I remember him, so of course he will. I haven't changed that much."

"Honey, you need to be on the floor and he's bound to see you then."

"I – I can work from the control room. That way I'll be out of sight." She paced. "He can't see me!"

"But I thought you wanted a relationship with him back then. Maybe he felt the same way. Don't you want to know?"

"It's been too long and it's complicated now. A lot of things in my life have changed since then."

Rachelle gave her friend a solemn look. "It doesn't have to be complicated, hon." She stood up and walked over to Prue, placing a comforting hand on her shoulder.

"You could talk to him. Find out how he feels. Who knows, he might've fallen for you too."

"No. I can't. It's too late for that. He's probably married or engaged or divorced, which makes it worse."

"He's not married. He lives in coastal California with two Rottweilers named Benji and Rocky."

Prue frowned at her.

Rachelle shrugged. "It's in his Bio."

Gabe came to the door. "What's going on? Why aren't you waiting for Mr. Colton?"

Rachelle glowered at him. "Prue's not feeling well. Can you do the meet and greet? I'll look after our girl and get her to the control room."

Gabe looked dazed for a moment. "Oh. Ok." He glanced at Prue and said, "Sorry you're not feeling well, lovely." Then he gazed along the corridor. "All right, I got this. See you on set." He strutted off down the passage.

"Crisis averted." Rachelle gave a triumphant smile.

Prue looked flustered. "Is it?" She hoped she wouldn't run into the author after his interview. The only way to avoid him was to hide in the control room until the recordings finished, and that's just what she planned to do.

Later that evening, at home in her apartment, Prue was grateful she had managed to avoid Nicholas Colton. Rachelle was probably right. A one night stand all those years ago would have been the last thing on the author's mind. He was famous. That was his focus now, why would he even be the least bit interested in her and her life?

Her mind wandered back to that night in the luxury hotel suite when he had been so attentive and affectionate. The way his hands had caressed and teased her body, and his mouth had taken hers with so much passion. She thought there had been more to the way he'd made love to her, but she hadn't dared to hope, and afterward, the way he'd looked at her across the room as though he wanted to say something. Had he felt the same?

She shook her head to clear the image from her mind. None of it mattered now. He'd walked away without telling her how he felt and she'd been guilty of doing the same. And when it came down to it, they had agreed to one night without any emotional strings, so why would she think it could have been anything more?

The doorbell rang, pulling her out of her thoughts. She wiped her wet hands on her apron, left the dishes in the sink and walked into her entry hall. Her heart trembled as she approached the front door, and she peered through the peephole to see who was there before opening it. She breathed a relieved sigh when she caught sight of the blonde waves and unlocked the door. "It's after eight, isn't it time for your beauty sleep?" she joked.

Rachelle held up a bottle of Pinot Noir and smiled. "I come bearing gifts." She brushed past Prue and entered the apartment. "Thought you could use a little drink."

Prue closed the door and followed her into the kitchen. "Thanks, but I'm fine."

Her friend walked over to a cupboard above the stove and took out two wine glasses. "You had a tough day today, honey. It's the least I can do. What are friends for?"

"I appreciate that, but I really am fine."

Rachelle grimaced. "You may not be after I tell you the news."

"What news?" Prue frowned and folded her arms.

"Nick's coming in tomorrow to deliver signed copies of his latest book. Isn't that sweet?" She poured the Pinot Noir and handed a glass to Prue. "After doing it for the audience he thought it would be a nice gesture to do the same for our staff."

"Nick? You're calling him Nick now?"

"He asked me to. Nicholas is his official author name he doesn't use it in person."

Prue swallowed a large mouthful of wine and coughed as the warm liquid slid into her queasy stomach. "Couldn't he have the books sent over by courier? Why does he have to hand-deliver them himself?"

"Because he's not a pretentious prick and wants to do something nice for everyone. The ladies at reception told him how much they loved his books."

"And what am I supposed to do? Hide out in the control room every day?" She plonked the wine glass onto the counter and strutted into the living room.

Rachelle followed her, glass in hand. "You might consider talking to him…"

Prue swung around. "You know I can't. I don't want to complicate my life by letting him into it. He had his chance, we both did, and we let it slip away."

"Honey, you can't hide from him forever."

"Yes I can. He lives on the other side of the country so it should be easy."

"What if he finds you one day?"

"There's no way he can unless someone tells him where I am." It sounded like an accusation, even to her.

Rachelle's expression darkened. "I hope you're not implying that I'd tell him."

Prue shook her head. "Of course not…"

A tiny voice echoed into the room. "Mommy, I'm thirsty." A little girl with curly brown hair, clad in pink Minnie Mouse pajamas, appeared in the doorway, rubbing sleepy eyes.

"Ok, sweetie. One sip and then back to bed." Prue took her daughter's hand.

"Ok, Mommy."

Rachelle waved to the little girl, blew her a kiss, then sat down on the off white sofa and swallowed the rest of her wine. She did understand why Prue was cautious, even though she thought it might be beneficial for Colton and his daughter to get to know each other. At least he wasn't a dead beat dad. He was successful and could offer them a better lifestyle, if only Prue could see it that way. But who was she to interfere? They were besties, and she had to support her friend no matter what she decided.

Prue returned to the living room after tucking her little girl back into bed. "She's asleep already." She sat down next to her friend. "She's the reason I can't see him. I can't disrupt her life because I have feelings for a man I slept with once."

Rachelle reached across and took her hand. "I understand that, but think of the child support." She grinned. "I'm joking. Kind of."

"I know." Prue gave a thin smile.

"Have you thought that he might be excited about having a child?"

"He's a famous author, renowned worldwide. Do you think a child would be in his plans? Come on, who are we kidding here?"

"Honey, he is a nice man." She squeezed her friend's hand.

Prue sighed. "Doesn't matter. I'm not prepared to upset Nikki's life by being selfish."

"Selfish? You? Are you serious? You're the most *not* selfish person I know. And that's saying something." She hugged her friend.

"Thanks, I think." Prue stood up and headed to the kitchen to retrieve the bottle of Pinot Noir.

When she returned she topped up Rachelle's glass and poured more into her own. She raised her glass. "To keeping secrets."

Rachelle eyed her with suspicion and raised her glass. "What, exactly, does that mean?"

"You keep my secret and I'll keep yours." She gave her a devious grin.

"That's blackmail, you know."

"Precisely."

_T_hree

The consensus in the control room at 10.30 was Starbucks coffee and blueberry scones for morning break. Prue had taken down everyone's order, called the cab company and was about to leave when Rachelle pulled her up. "Don't forget the Sweet 'N Low, hon," the TV host reminded. "Gotta watch my figure." She grinned.

"Already on it. And your figure's fine." Prue took the stairs to the ground floor and headed for the revolving door. The cab was already out front. She made her way to the glass turnstile and spotted Nicholas Colton on the sidewalk trying to maneuver a large box of books into the triangular space between the doors.

When Prue caught sight of him she stopped in her tracks. Could she make it to the taxi via the side door without him noticing her? He looked preoccupied with his difficult task so she was prepared to give it a try. She dashed over to the door on the left, pushed it open, rushed across the sidewalk, pulled open the cab door and dove in head first, sinking down in the seat so she wouldn't be seen. "Can we please go?" she asked.

The driver pulled out into the traffic shaking his head. His eyes met hers in the rearview mirror. "What's your problem, lady?"

Prue straightened in the seat, brushed an errant strand of blonde hair off her face, and sat her purse on her lap. "No problem."

While the taxi made its way to Columbus Circle, Prue worried about how she would get back into the building without being seen by the author. The main foyer could be a catastrophe. Maybe by the time she arrived he'd be gone. He was there only to drop off books, after all. How long could it take?

When the cab arrived at Starbucks, the driver turned into W 59th Street and parked, keeping the engine and meter running. Prue crossed at the pedestrian crossing, and entered the corner café. The place was cram-packed, as usual. She stood in line, checking her watch every couple of minutes. Why hadn't she thought to call ahead? The only benefit of it taking a while was that Nicholas should be gone by the time she got back to the broadcast center and that would be worth the wait.

Prue thought about him while she waited. How strange that she'd named her little girl Nicole. Did she have a sixth sense about the author? She wondered what his middle name was. She had chosen Grace after her maternal grandmother for Nikki's middle name. When she reached the counter she handed the order to the girl and was told it would take about ten to fifteen minutes. Prue paid, then moved to one of the tall, standing room only tables and checked her phone. Maybe Rachelle would text her when Nicholas was gone.

Heading back in the taxi, Prue's stomach tightened into a knot of prickling nerves. She had to avoid Nicholas Colton at all costs. She had no intention of complicating her life or his. And she knew if they met that's exactly what would happen. What would be the point after all these years, anyway?

Gabe was on the street, and as the cab pulled into the curb he opened the door and climbed in next to Prue. "Can you pull around back, please?" he asked the driver. "Make a left into 11th and another left into West 56th and pull up outside the second door."

Flicking on the indicator, the driver eased out onto the road, made a U-turn and followed Gabe's instructions.

"What's going on?" Prue asked.

"The author's still in the building and Rachelle asked me to take you through the back."

Prue felt her face grow warm and knew her cheeks were flushed. She was so angry with Rachelle. Even if she hadn't explained it to Gabe, he would be wondering. "Did Rachelle tell you why?"

Gabe wasn't good at hiding the truth. He gave her an awkward sideways glance. "Not exactly. She said you needed to keep a low profile while Nicholas Colton was here, so that's what we're doing."

"And what do you think she meant by that?"

He shrugged. "I don't know. I'm just doing what I was told to do, like a good little CBS employee."

"You must have some idea."

Gabe turned to her and folded his arms. "Ok, here's what I think. You and the author had a romantic tryst at some point and you don't want to see him."

Prue gave a heavy sigh. "Something like that."

The taxi pulled up at the single black door.

"You don't have to worry, lovely one, I've got your back." He took her hand in his and smiled. "Let's get these coffees to the control room before they go cold, or neither one of us will be popular."

When Gabe and Prue reached the busy workroom everyone cheered. "Coffee!" The pair passed the drinks and scones around then sat up the back to watch the rest of Rachelle's show, only half an hour to go for the first recording. Prue wondered where Nicholas was. If he was still in the building, she figured he'd be waiting in Rachelle's office until the first show finished. She thought about asking Gabe to take a look. She needed to know where the author was so they didn't run into each other.

"Gabe?" she whispered.

He turned, sighed, and eyed her with a frown. "What do you want me to do?"

It was funny how he always knew when she was going to ask him to run an errand for her.

"Do you think Nicholas Colton is waiting in Rachelle's office?"

"Why? Want me to go check?" He folded his arms.

Prue gave him her sweetest smile. "Would you mind? I'd really appreciate it."

Gabe sighed again. "Even if I do mind I'm still going. The suspense is killing me." He stood up. "Back in a few."

She smiled up at him. "Thank you."

Ted Cook, the production manager shushed them.

"Sorry," Prue said. She sat in silence and watched the monitors, her stomach tight as a drum. The stress of having the author in the building and the risk of running into him was too much for her to cope with.

Gabe was back within minutes. He entered the control room, sidled into the seat beside Prue, and whispered in her ear, "He's there."

She sighed. "I hope Rachelle takes the books and sends him on his way. I need to go pick up…" She realized she couldn't tell Gabe about Nikki. It would be too obvious. She had to pick her daughter up from preschool.

"Pick up?" He looked at her with an eyebrow raised.

"Some groceries from the market."

Gabe patted her knee. "The market's open till 9.00, lovely. You should be fine."

The afternoon's recording finished in no time, and when the credits rolled everyone removed their headsets, stood up and stretched. "Great show!" they each said, gathering up their belongings to leave.

Prue remained seated, Gabe beside her. She wasn't ready to walk out the door and straight into Nicholas Colton. She could only hope he'd left between takes.

Ted walked over to them. "We're closing up shop."

"Would it be alright if we stayed for a few more minutes? I'll lock up," Prue promised.

"Everything ok?" Ted asked.

"Yes, everything's fine." She didn't want to elaborate. "I need to talk to Gabe in private for a minute, that's all."

"Ok, see you Monday. Have a great weekend." He made his way over to the door and left.

That's right. It was Friday. The weekend was here. Prue sighed with relief. At least she wouldn't run the risk of bumping into the author in her neighborhood. And, besides, wouldn't he be heading back to California? Or on to his next interview or book signing?

Once the control room cleared, Prue asked Gabe to check if the author had left. When he returned he told her Nicholas had waited to offer personal messages in each book. Prue gave a huffy sigh. Why couldn't he just sign them and leave it at that? How was she going to get out of the building without him seeing her? Gabe suggested taking the way they had come in with the coffee.

Prue kissed his cheek. "You're a genius!"

Gabe blushed. "Thanks. Glad someone appreciates my talents."

The taxi was outside the door when Gabe walked Prue out. "Have a stressless weekend, lovely."

"Thanks. You too." She gave him a hug and stepped into the cab.

When the taxi turned into W 57th and drove past the front entrance of the building, the author appeared on the sidewalk with Rachelle.

Prue ducked back in the seat so she wouldn't be seen and hoped it would be the last time she laid eyes on Nicholas Colton.

$\mathcal{F}$our

Two uneventful months went by and Prue was happy. No Nicholas Colton to deal with and no major dramas either. What more could she ask for? Her job was going well and she enjoyed working with the people in her team. They were a great fit. And she'd been noticed by CBS management, which was a plus. Maybe a promotion would be coming her way soon. At least she could dream.

The holiday season was fast-approaching, with Halloween right around the corner and only ten weeks until Christmas. Her daughter was excited that Santa was on his way. She had already given Prue several choices for gifts. Christmas was a wonderful time of year. Prue especially loved getting into the holiday spirit by decorating and baking.

Nikki had asked when they were going to see her grandma, she had been asking since they arrived in New York. They both missed the family, but even so, it had been an important move and Prue didn't regret the decision. She wanted a better life for herself and her daughter and working in New York would achieve that. She loved the television industry. It had always been her dream to work on a show like Rachelle's and when the opportunity presented itself she took it.

Her mother had called last week to ask if her girls were coming home for the holidays. She missed them and hoped they could make the trip. Prue wasn't sure about making any definite plans because the vacation roster hadn't been posted at work yet. She told her mom she would do her best, which was all she could offer. Nikki had been on the phone with her grandma for over an hour, giggling and telling her all about her new school and friends. Prue knew how much spending time with her grandparents meant to Nikki, and she *would* make every effort to arrange some vacation time so they could go back home for the holidays.

Her daughter was in the living room playing Go Fish with her new best friend, Jacinta. She was glad her little girl had settled into her new preschool and had made some new friends. It made being in a new city that much easier for the both of them.

Prue had just put dinner in the oven when the doorbell rang. She took off her apron and made a beeline for the entry hall. Nikki and Jacinta jumped up off the floor and ran to open the door before Prue could ask them to wait until she checked to see who was outside. When the girls swung the door back, Jacinta's mom was in the hall. The little girl wrapped her arms around her mother's hips and bear-hugged her. "I love you, Momma."

"I love you too, sweetheart," her mom said, leaning down to pull her daughter into her arms.

Prue smiled. "Got time for coffee?"

Yolanda picked up her baby girl. "Wish I could but I gotta work tonight."

"Ok. Next time?"

"Absolutely." She kissed her daughter's cheek. "Say goodnight to Nikki, honey. We have to go."

Jacinta waved. "See ya tomorrow."

Nikki waved back. "See ya."

After dinner, Prue got her daughter ready for bed, tucked her in, then snuggled under a bright pink throw rug on the sofa and turned on the television. She flicked through a dozen channels before stopping at the day's rerun of The Ellen DeGeneres Show. She loved watching it but didn't get the chance very often because it aired during the day, so this was a treat. She loved the style of the show. It was relaxed and quirky, which made it fun and entertaining. Rachelle's show, on the other hand, was more analytical to Prue's mind. It had great guests and offered an informative view but didn't have the same entertainment factor.

Prue dashed into the kitchen to make a cup of hot chocolate during the last couple of minutes before the ad break and when she returned to her seat she was surprised to hear that Nicholas Colton was up next. Couldn't she escape the man even in her own home?

She was about to flick to another channel when the TV host gave a brief intro of his latest release, One Night of Passion. Prue's stomach shrank. *He writes thrillers, doesn't he? What is this book about?* She sat the remote on the coffee table and settled back on the sofa to watch the segment. Could he have written about their night together?

When Nicholas walked on stage, waving to the excited audience, who gave him a standing ovation, the heater under Prue's window clattered and the ceiling light flickered. She heard an electrical buzz and the room went dark.

"No! No, no, no." Prue felt around the coffee table for her iPhone and snatched it up. She pressed the button and swiped the face. "Why now? I wanted to watch that."

She jumped off the sofa and used the flashlight app to make her way down the short hallway to her daughter's bedroom. She opened the door and peered inside. Nikki was sound asleep. Good.

Prue headed to the front door, unlocked the deadlock, removed the chain, and opened it. Other tenants were outside their apartments with their cell phones in hand complaining to each other about the outage. Duane, Yolanda's husband, came along the hall and handed her a battery operated lantern. "Here, this might be useful for a while. The manager doesn't know how long it'll take to get the power back on. Is Nikki ok?"

"Yes, she's sleeping like a baby, thank goodness."

Duane nodded. "That's good. Mine too." He turned to walk away.

"Thanks for this," she said, holding up the lantern. "I appreciate it."

He waved it off. "No problem. Better get back to Jazz and Sammy. Catch you later."

Prue locked her door. She was grateful for neighbors like Yolanda and Duane. They were good people.

She wondered how long it would take for the power to come back on. She wanted to find out what Nicholas' book was about. She followed the bright light of her phone back into the living room and plonked herself down on the sofa with a huff. *Why did the power have to go out now?* Could the author have written a novel about their liaison? It made her insides quiver.

By the time the power was restored, the talk show host was thanking her guests and gave a special mention about One Night of Passion being available at Barnes and Noble and other leading bookstores. Prue made a mental note to pick up a copy. She needed to know what was in that novel.

Five

When Prue arrived at work the next morning, Rachelle rushed up to her in the corridor all smiles. With the holiday season almost upon them she'd had an epiphany. She asked Prue if she could get someone to babysit Nikki from Friday night to Sunday so they could have a girls' weekend Christmas shopping in Los Angeles. It had been a few years since she'd been there and it would be a great break.

Prue ran the idea around her mind. It would be a wonderful break, and she hadn't been to LA before. Would her neighbor mind her daughter? "I'll have to ask Yolanda if she wouldn't mind having Nikki for a couple of days before I can say yes. But I'd love to come, if I can."

"Great. You organize that and I'll do the rest." Rachelle rushed off down the corridor to her office. She was a woman on a mission. The weekend was shaping up to be a lot of fun.

Gabe came up to Prue with the morning's schedule and handed her the clipboard. "Why does Rachelle look like the cat that swallowed the canary?"

Prue frowned at him. "Gabe! That's not nice."

"Well she does." He folded his arms. "What's she up to anyway?"

"She's planning a Christmas shopping weekend for the two of us, that's all." She ran her eyes over the sheet of paper on the clipboard. "Why are you so suspicious?"

He pressed his hand to his chest and gave her a look of indignation. "Moi? Suspicious? How can you think such a thing? I thought we were best buds."

"We're not best buds, we're co-conspirators." She giggled.

Gabe chuckled. "You're right about that one, sweetie." He started to walk away, then turned around. "Please be careful. Rachelle's plans have been known to backfire with serious consequences. That's all I'm saying." He continued down the corridor.

Prue's eyes followed him. What did he mean by that? Was he being facetious? What could possibly go wrong on a shopping weekend?

Later in the morning, Prue gave Yolanda a quick call. Her neighbor was more than happy to have Nikki sleep over for the weekend. She even suggested that she drop the girls at preschool on Monday so Prue could prepare for work without having to rush to organize things for the beginning of the school week. Prue thanked her and, once off the phone, decided she would have to do something nice for Yolanda. Maybe they could see a movie together or have lunch some time, or both.

After the call, Prue went to tell the TV host that she could make the trip. When she reached Rachelle's office her friend was on the phone. Prue waited outside the glass wall until Rachelle finished the call and waved her in. "So how did it go? Are we off to LA?"

Prue sat down in the chair in front of Rachelle's desk. "All arranged. I can't wait."

"I knew you'd manage it so I booked our flights." She spun her laptop around. "We're leaving at 3.31 p.m. Friday afternoon on Virgin Atlantic. And don't worry I've already cleared it with management so we can leave early."

Prue shook her head. "How do you do it?"

Rachelle smiled. "I do have some influence around here. At least some of the time." She winked.

"You amaze me."

"Thanks. I amaze me too." Rachelle's smile widened. She came around the desk and hugged her friend. "We're going to have a ball!"

"I haven't had a vacation in," she thought about it, "a really long time. I'm so looking forward to it."

"I got us a suite at Hilton Checkers, in the downtown Financial District, so we're right in the thick of it. LA Live, the fashion district, great restaurants and tourist attractions. It's going to be *amazing*."

Prue sighed with happiness. "Sounds wonderful."

Gabe poked his head around the door. "Ladies, please, let's hustle. We've got a show to do."

Rachelle waved him off. "Shoo. We'll be there in five."

He gave her an annoyed frown and strutted off down the corridor, saying "Diva" under his breath.

"Before we go, I wanted to give you this." Rachelle walked around her desk, opened the top drawer and took out a copy of Nicholas' novel. "Thought you'd want to read it."

Prue took the book and gazed at the cover and the title, *One Night of Passion*. Yes, she did want to read it. She needed to know if he remembered their night together and if that's what he'd written about, or was she looking for something that wasn't there?

She turned the book over and stared at his handsome face. "I planned to pick up a copy from Barnes and Noble on the weekend as I didn't get one when he dropped them off. Thank you for saving this for me."

"It's the least I could do for my bestie?" She gave her an uncertain smile. "Do you think it is about you?"

"I won't know until I read it. Maybe." She popped the book into her purse and headed for the door. "Coming? We have to hustle, remember?"

Rachelle waved the comment off. "Oh, Gabe is such a girl. We've got heaps of time." She looped her arm through Prue's and they stepped out into the corridor and headed for the studio. "We are going to have so much fun in LA. I can't wait to show you around."

Six

At 3 p.m. Friday afternoon, Prue and Rachelle were waiting at JFK Airport's Terminal 4 to board their flight. Both women were excited about their weekend shopping expedition and couldn't wait to be on the plane and in air. Prue had packed light, thinking she might pick up a few new things for herself and Nikki in the fashion district. Rachelle had over packed and Prue wondered where her friend planned to put all the shopping she was going to do.

The call to board their flight to Los Angeles was announced over the PA system and the pair popped out of their seats, gathered their belongings and joined the queue. At last they were on their way.

Once on board, Prue by the window, they made themselves comfortable for the five and a half hour flight.

Rachelle had picked up some magazines while they were waiting and both women flipped through the glossy pages until the announcement was made to put everything away ready for takeoff.

It was going to be a late night. By the time they landed, got through security, and found a taxi it would be after 11 p.m., but they didn't care, the weekend was going to be so much fun. They planned an early start on Saturday so they could take in some sights as well as go shopping.

When the taxi pulled up outside their hotel both women were ready to fall into bed. The driver had been very helpful with information about where to shop and eat and how to stay safe in the city. He helped them with their luggage and Rachelle gave him a large tip.

The hotel lobby was opulent, and Prue gazed around at her elegant surroundings. Double red wood and ivory marble-topped reception desk to the left, curtained bar and lounge to the right. Polished, cream and black tile floors and gold framed mirrors adorned the walls. It took her breath away.

The night manager said he had all the information he needed and handed them their swipe keys. He directed them to the elevators and hoped they enjoyed their stay in Los Angeles.

Inside their hotel suite, Prue and Rachelle readied themselves for bed. It had been a long flight and getting through security had taken longer than expected. After a good night's sleep they'd be ready to put in a full day of shopping and fun.

The next morning, Prue woke early. She wanted to give Nikki a call before she and Rachelle headed downstairs for breakfast. She grabbed her cell phone from her purse and snuck into the living room so she wouldn't wake her friend. Yolanda answered her cell phone half asleep. "Hi. It's 4 a.m. here," she whispered. "I guess you forgot about the three hour time difference, huh?" Prue apologized profusely for waking her up.

When Nikki came to the phone she was sleepy but happy to hear her mom's voice and asked if she was having fun. Prue told her they hadn't left the hotel yet, but when they did she would take some photos and message them to Yolanda for her.

Nikki told her mom she loved her. Prue gave her daughter a kiss through the phone, said "I love you," ended the call and returned to the bedroom.

Rachelle was still sound asleep with a pink satin and black lace mask covering her eyes. Prue wasn't sure if she should wake her up, but if she didn't they'd be late going down for breakfast and getting the early start they wanted.

She wandered over to Rachelle's bed and wriggled her foot. "Rachelle," she whispered, "you awake?"

Her friend stirred and gave a soft snort but didn't answer.

Prue bit her bottom lip. Should she try again?

She gave Rachelle's foot a firm tug. "Rachelle? We wanted to get an early start, remember?"

Rachelle flopped onto her back and lifted one corner of the eye mask. "What time is it?" she asked through a sleepy sigh.

Prue checked the clock radio. "A little after seven."

"Seven?!" Rachelle threw back the covers and scrambled out of bed. "Give me ten minutes and I'll be ready to go." She unzipped her suitcase, found what she planned to wear and headed to the bathroom.

While Rachelle was closeted in the bathroom, which could take longer than ten minutes, Prue changed into the outfit she'd chosen to wear and applied some makeup. She didn't want to overdo it she wanted to keep her look fresh and light.

Rachelle emerged from the bathroom twenty minutes later wearing a brunette wig and looking ready and raring to go. Prue was surprised by the new look. "Best I go incognito. Don't want to be stopped by fans every five minutes. After breakfast, I think we'll head to Macy's. They have a sale on and we're sure to find some bargains there. Did Nikki put in her Christmas order yet?"

"Yes, she did. She'd love a Discovery Kids Laptop Computer. She said she wants to be like me. Oh, and a minion from the movie Despicable Me." She giggled.

Rachelle smiled. "That's so sweet." She grabbed a jacket from her case and picked up her purse. "Well, let's eat so we can get going."

"Great idea. I'm starved."

The doorman opened the door for the ladies, tipped his hat and said good morning. He also informed them that their rental car was out front and handed Rachelle the remote key. When she pressed it, he walked over and opened the door closest to the sidewalk. He recognized the TV host even in her hairpiece and mentioned that his wife loved her show and it was such a treat to meet her. Rachelle told him to please say hello for her and that she was so happy to meet the husband of a fan. He said he would definitely do that and told them to have a nice day in LA.

"When did you arrange this?" Prue asked, climbing into the plush passenger seat and fastening her seatbelt.

"I organized it when I made the hotel reservation. I didn't think we'd want to traipse around in a taxi all day. At least this way we can go wherever we want without having to wait." Rachelle fastened her seatbelt and started the engine. "Macy's here we come!" She eased the classic white Audi A3 into the traffic and headed for the department store which was only a few minutes away.

Once they found a spot in the parking garage, they made their way into the complex.

The Bloc, once Macy's Plaza, looked so different now that the renovations were almost complete. Some stores and a couple of cafés were located in an outdoor courtyard, giving the center an al fresco feel. Prue wanted to go straight to Macy's toy department to buy Nikki's Christmas gifts first. She didn't want to miss out on getting exactly what her little girl had asked for. After all, Santa didn't make that kind of mistake. When they were done, the pair headed to the women's fashion section to see what was on sale.

They gathered up the clothes they'd chosen and took them to the fitting room. Prue hadn't done anything like this in a long time and was having so much fun. Each one tried on an outfit then came out to show the other. If something looked off they'd both giggle like school girls.

After trying on a few outfits, Rachelle appeared in her own clothes. "Sorry, hon, I have to pee. Must've been all those cups of coffee at breakfast. Will you be ok till I get back?"

Prue bundled up the clothes she wanted to buy. "Of course. You go. I'll meet you at the men's cologne counter. I want to pick up something for my dad and my brother."

"Ok." Rachelle rushed off to find the restroom.

While her friend was gone, Prue paid for the clothing, then wandered through the store to the men's aftershave. The aroma of cologne lingered in the air around her as customers sprayed sample bottles to see if they liked the smell. One heady fragrance prodded her nostrils and took her mind back to that night with Nicholas. He had smelled so good.

She made her way to an empty section of the counter and perused the assortment of testers. What would her dad like? And what about her brother, Toby? She selected a bottle of Hugo Boss, sprayed a small amount onto a card, then sniffed. Neither her brother nor her dad would wear that one.

Prue ran her eyes over the bottles again and chose Burberry Touch. She loved the intimacy the name evoked.

Not bad, but still not quite right for the rugged men in the Granger family. She sprayed a couple of Gucci fragrances and thought they were nice, but wasn't sure if her dad or her brother would feel the same. She sighed. It was harder than she thought it would be.

A male voice beside her said, "Difficult to find just the right one, isn't it?"

"Yes, it is." Prue returned the bottle to its place and turned her head.

"It's you!" The expression on Nicholas' face was one of pleasant surprise.

Prue felt her heart drop into her stomach. How could this happen? Her cheeks flushed. "Hello. I didn't expect to see you here." *What am I saying?*

"I never expected to see you again, but I'm glad I have." He couldn't take his eyes off her. She was still as lovely as he remembered. "Do you live in LA?"

Prue shook her head. "No. I'm here on vacation, uh … with a friend." She gave him a thin smile.

"I see." His smile disappeared, the look of disappointment evident on his face.

He thought she was in Los Angeles with a man and she wasn't about to dissuade him. As much as she wanted to she couldn't let him into her life now.

They stood staring into each other's eyes for a moment until Prue regained her muddled senses. "I – I must go. My friend will be waiting for me. It's been good seeing you again."

"Yes, it's been good seeing you too." Nicholas held out his hand.

Prue hesitated before placing her hand in his. Her mind wandered back to that night and how his gentle fingers had roamed her body so intimately, giving her so much pleasure. Her heart trembled when their palms connected and her face grew warmer.

Nicholas didn't want to let her go, but when she glanced at her watch he knew it was his cue to leave. Another man was waiting for her. "Take care of yourself, won't you?"

"Yes. You too."

Nicholas Colton turned and walked out of her life for the second time.

Seven

Prue scrambled through the department store, her mind in a flurry, searching for Rachelle. She asked a staff member where the restroom was and made a beeline for the second floor. Rushing into the ladies, she called for her friend. "Rachelle? Rachelle, are you here?" she said, breathless. No answer. *Where could she be?*

She hurried out of the bathroom and headed back downstairs to the fitting room. Perhaps Rachelle had gone back to collect the outfits she wanted to buy. Prue dashed into the room. The cubicles were empty. She hunted through her purse for her cell phone, snatched it out of the bag and pressed the button. There were two missed calls from Rachelle. Why hadn't she heard the musical tone? Because she had been too preoccupied with Nicholas Colton, that's why.

Prue dialed her friend's cell. Voicemail kicked in. Out of frustration, she dropped her phone back into her purse and gazed around the store, scanning the different sections for Rachelle. No sign of her. Where was her friend?

Someone tapped her on the shoulder and she swung around. "Where have you been? I've been looking for you everywhere," she said, her voice strained.

Rachelle grimaced. "I had a migraine coming on so I went to find a drug store. I did try to call." She placed a comforting hand on Prue's arm. "Are you ok, hon? You look frazzled."

"No, I'm not ok." She changed the heavy bags on her right arm to her left. "I ran into Nicholas Colton. Or rather he ran into me. At the men's cologne counter."

Rachelle's eyes widened. "What?" She glanced over her shoulder. "Where is he now?"

"Gone, I hope." She brushed stray strands of her blonde hair from her flushed face. "I can't believe he was here. I can't believe we spoke to each other after all this time."

"Why don't we go get a coffee and take a break?" Rachelle looped her arm through Prue's. "There's a café on the street."

Prue nodded and they headed along the walkway to the front of the complex.

Rachelle ordered the drinks then joined Prue at their table. "Feeling any better?"

Prue wasn't sure how she felt. She had to keep reminding herself that not having Nicholas Colton in her life was the best thing for her and her daughter. But she realized she still had feelings for the man. A man who had made passionate love to her all those years ago. Why wouldn't those feelings go away? Even though he fathered her child it didn't mean she had to hold on to the emotions she felt back then, did it? "No. I've done everything I can to avoid Nicholas since he arrived at the studio, and now I run into him here of all places. How can that happen?"

"Serendipity," Rachelle told her, a whimsical expression on her face. "I'm a big believer of fate, you know."

Their coffee arrived and Rachelle took a cautious sip.

Prue looked into her friend's eyes. "Do you really believe that? Do you think we were destined to meet?" She stirred a sachet of sugar into her latte.

Rachelle leaned forward and rested her elbows on the table. "You're connected to him through Nikki. It was bound to happen sooner or later."

Prue frowned. "She's the reason I don't want to complicate things. I can't have her life turned upside down now. It wouldn't be fair."

Her friend reached across the table and squeezed her hand. "I know, but what are you going to do about how you feel? You can't run away from your heart forever."

"Yes, I can. I have to. I'm a mom first, my feelings don't matter. I have to protect my daughter. I won't let her be hurt." A tear slid down Prue's cheek and she brushed it away.

"Honey, you deserve to be happy too. What if he's the one who can do that?"

Prue sniffed back the urge to cry. "Can we please not talk about it anymore? Let's just enjoy our coffee and the rest of the day. Ok?"

Rachelle gave her a pained frown and squeezed her hand again. "If that's what you want."

Prue nodded. "It is." Although she couldn't get the look of disappointment on Nicholas' face out of her mind when she'd told him she was with a friend.

When Nicholas arrived at his parked car he stopped and glanced over his shoulder. Why had he walked away from her again? Why hadn't he asked her to have coffee with him? He knew the reason. She was with another man and he had no right to ask anything of her.

He pressed the button on the remote and climbed into his black BMW, closed the door and sat gazing out of the windshield, his mind wandering back to that night in Pittsburgh. They had made love to each other as though they were in love. By the time it had come to an end he realized he was in love with her. Foolish, he knew, to give his heart away so easily. But it had been a long time since his wife had passed away, and she always told him if anything happened to her he should find someone else to love, he was a good man who deserved to be loved. At the time, he hadn't wanted to think about it and told her he would only ever love her. A promise he'd planned to keep.

It had been three solitary years when he'd met the lovely young woman who had shared herself body and soul with him, and he had always wondered about her. What she was doing. Was she happy? Why had he walked out of that hotel room without telling her how he felt? How could he be so stupid to walk away from her a second time? He gave a heavy sigh. *Could she still be in the store? Could I have a second chance?*

Nicholas opened the car door and stepped out. He had to find her, had to know if she felt the same way. He locked his sedan and hurried back into the complex. Making his way past shoppers to Macy's entrance he rushed through the department store to the men's collection. She wasn't there.

He wandered through women's fashion and thought he caught a glimpse of her, but when he got closer he could see it wasn't her. His heart turned to lead in his chest. She was gone and he would never know her name or anything else about her.

Eight

It had been four weeks since she'd run into Nicholas at Macy's and Prue couldn't get him out of her mind, no matter how hard she tried. She had done everything she could to keep her feelings locked away, but seeing him again had changed all that. Prue knew it was silly to feel the way she did after only one night, but she couldn't help it. Her heart wouldn't allow her to forget him.

She plonked herself down on the sofa with a sigh, turned on the TV and lowered the volume. It was almost 12.40 a.m. and she couldn't sleep, so rather than toss and turn for hours she decided to do something constructive. She flicked through the various channels and stopped at a late night talk show. At least she was keeping up with the other New York television networks top-rating talk shows, so technically she was working.

After watching the show for half an hour Prue got up to make herself a cup of warm milk and honey during the ad break. She hoped it would relax her enough so she could go to back to bed and get some sleep. Thank goodness it was Sunday morning. She could attempt a sleep in, if Nikki didn't wake up at the crack of dawn. Wishful thinking, she knew.

Prue sat cross-legged with the warm mug in her hands and waited for the last couple of commercials to finish. When the show returned she was shocked to see the talk show host hold up a copy of Nicholas' book and introduce the author. He was getting a lot of air time for this particular novel. Maybe now she would find out what it was about as she hadn't had a chance to read it yet.

"Let's give a warm welcome to award-winning, New York Times and USA Today's bestselling author Nicholas Colton." He stood, walked over to the author and shook his hand, then both men moved across to the host's desk and sat down. "Welcome. It's good to have you on the show."

"Thanks for having me. It's great to be here."

"So, Nicholas…"

"Please, call me Nick. Nicholas is too formal and only used for my novels." He crossed one leg over the other and unbuttoned his jacket in an attempt to alleviate his nerves. He couldn't get used to being in the spotlight no matter how many times he appeared on a talk show.

"Ok. Nick, your latest book is different to your regular format." He held up the copy again. "A romantic thriller? That's kind of off base for you, isn't it?"

Nicholas chuckled. "Yes, I suppose you could say that. It was something I've had simmering in the back of my mind for a few years now and I felt it was time to put it down on paper."

"Can you tell the viewers something about the plot?"

"Sure." He turned to look at the audience. "A couple meets in a bar and decides to have a one night stand. Neither one has been in a relationship for quite a while and realizes they need to feel desired, no matter how brief the encounter. Unbeknown to them, they're being watched by a psychopathic serial killer who has been stalking the woman for several weeks." He smiled. "Can't give too much away. Hopefully viewers will want to read the book to find out what happens."

"Yes, of course." He flicked through the pages. "So what was the inspiration behind this new storyline?"

Nicholas cleared his throat. "Well, some of it is based on fact and the rest is fiction."

Prue realized she'd been holding her breath while watching the author discuss his novel. She let out the huge rush of air, drank the last of her warm milk and flicked off the television. The book *was* about them ... with a thriller twist, of course. It had been simmering in his head for a few years? So he had been thinking about her too.

She sat the empty cup in the sink and padded down the hallway to her room.

At 3.06 a.m. Prue turned over, gave a heavy sigh, and glanced at the clock radio on her bedside table. Nicholas' interview kept playing over and over in her mind. He had written the book about their night together. She wondered how much 'fact', as he had worded it, was in the pages of that novel.

Prue flicked on the lamp, threw back the covers and swung her legs over the side of the bed, the soles of her feet sinking into the soft blue rug. She padded over to the closet, opened the door and pulled the book from the purse she had placed it in when Rachelle had given it to her. She turned the book over, gazed at Nicholas' handsome face smiling back at her and sighed.

She climbed back into bed, pulled the covers up around her, snuggled into the pillows and opened the book to the first page: Chapter One ~ The Rhythm of the Night.

At 6.05 a.m. Prue was awakened by her daughter tapping her on the arm. "Mommy, I'm hungry."

Prue turned over, opened her eyes and blinked a few times to clear away the haze of sleep. She had only slept for about an hour after reading for the entire night. "Morning, honey." She yawned and reached out to give her daughter a hug. "Mommy's still sleepy." She lifted the bedclothes. "Wanna climb in and snuggle for a while?"

Nikki shook her head. "My tummy's growling. Can I please have some Lucky Charms?"

Prue sighed and threw back the covers. Nicholas' novel slid off her bed and onto the rug. Nikki squatted, picked it up, stood and stared at the cover. "What's this story about, Mommy? Looks scary."

Not being the kind of thing she wanted her daughter exposed to, Prue reached out and took the novel from her hands. "It's a grown up book, sweetie. Not something little girls should be looking at." She smiled. "Ok. Let's go get you some breakfast." She sat the hard cover face down on her bedside table, took Nikki's hand and headed to the kitchen, glancing over her shoulder at the book as she stepped into the hall.

Prue and her daughter talked about their Halloween plans over breakfast. Nikki wanted a minion costume. She asked her mom what she wanted to be. Prue decided to dress up as Columbia from The Rocky Horror Picture Show. It was one of her favorite movies. She realized she would have to order the costumes online soon otherwise they might not arrive in time. This would be their first Halloween in The Big Apple and she hoped it would be a lot of fun for Nikki.

The telephone rang and Prue went to the kitchen to answer it. "Hello."

"Hi, it's me. I've scored four VIP tickets to the 8th Annual Lodge of Horror Halloween Bash at the Maple on Halloween Eve," Rachelle said, excited. "What are you going to wear?"

Prue sighed. She didn't want to go out for Halloween. She wanted to spend the time with Nikki, Yolanda, Jazz and Sammy trick-or-treating. But she realized that by the time the bash started the kids would be sound asleep. So there was no getting out of it. "I'm buying a Columbia costume online. Will that do?"

"Columbia? Who's that?"

"She's from The Rocky Horror Picture Show. Haven't you seen it?"

"Oh, of course I have. Love it. So avant-garde."

"So what do you think about the costume?"

"Yes, sounds perfect. I'll pick you up around nine thirty. Don't want to be the first to arrive."

"Let's talk about it tomorrow."

"Sure. It's going to be sooo much fun! See you in the morning."

"Bye." Prue hung up and rejoined her daughter at the breakfast table.

"Who was that, Mommy?"

"Aunty Rachelle. She's taking mommy out on Halloween Eve after we go trick-or-treating. We'll see if you can stay over at Jazz's."

Nikki beamed. "That'd be fun. I love staying over. Her mom makes waffles with maple syrup and ice cream for breakfast. Can I leave the table now, Mommy?" Prue nodded and Nikki took her bowl to the sink then ran off down the hallway to play in her room.

Prue grabbed her laptop from off the buffet and found several online costume stores in New York. She decided to go with New York Costumes and ordered hers and Nikki's outfits. She was relieved delivery would only take two to three business days. That meant they would arrive in plenty of time for Halloween.

Feeling exhausted after the long night, Prue shut her computer, stretched out on the sofa and closed her eyes.

Nine

Prue woke with a start to someone knocking on her front door. She gathered her sleepy senses and pushed herself up off the sofa. "Just a minute." She was about to walk out into the hall when Nikki ran down the hallway and pulled the door open. "Hello," she said, looking up at the man standing in their doorway. "You're very tall."

He smiled. "Am I? Well, thank you."

Nikki frowned at him. "Do you know m…?"

Prue came into the entry hall. "It's ok, honey. I'll talk to the man. You can go play now."

Nikki gave her mom a curious frown and remained where she was. "Why?"

"Because I asked you to." She pointed along the hallway. "Off you go, please."

Nikki turned around and skipped back to her room without another word.

"How did you find me?" Prue asked.

"That's not important. Why you didn't you tell me I had a daughter. Don't you think I had a right to know?"

Prue was stunned. She didn't understand how Nicholas could have found her without knowing her name or where she lived. "I'm not sure what you mean."

"The little girl, she's yours, isn't she? How old would she be? Five? Six? The numbers seem to add up, don't they?"

Prue stepped out into the hall and pulled the door closed. "Will you please keep your voice down? She's not your daughter. How did you find me?" she asked again.

"The day I was at the broadcast center delivering my books. You darted out of a side door and jumped into a cab. You thought I didn't see you, but I did."

"Why didn't you say anything when we met in LA?"

"Because at first I wasn't certain it was you that day. I had to be sure, so after seeing you in LA, I asked one of the receptionists. She told me your name, emailed me a picture of you, and here I am. It's not difficult finding an address when you have a surname to go by. Now tell me again she's not mine."

"How did you expect me to find you?" She folded her arms. "We didn't exactly exchange names when we exchanged bodily fluids, did we? I had no idea who you were until I saw you at the broadcast center."

"Why didn't you tell me then?" Why hide it from me?"

"We've been fine without you in our lives. I wasn't about to disrupt my daughter's life for your sake or mine."

"That's not fair." He folded his arms. "I could have been a part of her life from birth if you'd tried to find me."

"I didn't know how. Did you try to find me before now?"

"As a matter of fact, I did. But…"

"Exactly."

Right at that moment the door swung back. "Mommy, I'm thirsty. Can I please have a drink?"

Both Prue and Nicholas glanced at their little girl.

Nikki smiled up at the man standing with her mom. "Are you staying for dinner?"

"I don't think I'm invited."

"Why not?" She glanced at Prue. "Can he stay for dinner, Mommy?"

"He's busy, honey." Prue scooted her daughter into the kitchen. She turned to Nicholas and said, "Wait there."

70

Within minutes she was back at the door. "You have to leave."

"I have a right to get to know my daughter. I've already missed so much of her life."

She pushed him backwards. "Not now you don't."

He stepped up to her. "She needs to know she has a daddy. Are you going to deny her that?"

Nikki appeared in the hallway, her eyes brimming with tears. "Is… is he my daddy, Mommy?"

Prue jolted awake her heart racing. She sprang up into a sitting position, trying to gather her sleepy senses, and gazed around the living room. It took a few seconds for her to remember where she was. She glimpsed the wall clock and realized she'd been asleep for almost twenty minutes. She pulled herself up off the sofa and rushed down the hallway to Nikki's room. Her little girl was playing happily with the dolls in her dollhouse.

Prue gave a huge sigh of relief. Thank God it was only a dream.

Ten

In Rachelle's office the next morning, Prue told her all about her frightening dream. For once, the TV host sat and listened to every word without interruption, she could see how distressed her friend was. Prue paced as she relayed how Nicholas had appeared at her door and how Nikki had overheard him say he was her daddy. Rachelle came around the desk, and wrapped her arms around Prue. "It was a dream, hon. He hasn't found you. Nikki's ok."

Prue looked at her with tear-filled eyes. "But what if he does?" She brushed a tear from her cheek and sniffled. "I have to make sure he doesn't."

"How are you going to do that?" She walked Prue over to the sofa and sat down with her. "Look, he doesn't know your name or where you are, there's no way he *can* find you."

Prue gave a heavy sigh. "Logically, yes, but what if he figures out a way?"

Rachelle squeezed her hand. "Listen to me, ok. Think about it. How can he without any information?"

Prue popped up off the sofa and paced again. "I don't know, but he might. He's an author with connections." She turned around. "What if we run into each other again?"

Rachelle gave her a skeptical frown. "The chances of that happening are slim to none."

"What about Serendipity?" Prue stood with her hands on her hips.

"Well, there's that of course." She looked sheepish.

Prue plonked down on the sofa beside her. "See. It could happen. He travels interstate for his novel, so who's to say he doesn't do another book signing here somewhere and we run into each other again? What if Nikki's with me the next time?"

"Honey, you're letting your imagination run wild." She got up, walked around her desk and opened the bottom drawer. She took out two glasses and a bottle of Bourbon and poured a finger's breadth into each one, then returned the bottle to the drawer and kicked it shut with her stiletto-heeled foot. "Here." She passed a glass to Prue. "Drink up, it'll calm your nerves."

Prue sipped the honey-colored liquid and coughed as it slid into the tangle of butterflies in the pit of her stomach. "Thanks."

"No problem. You've got to pull yourself together, hon. You have a daughter to consider."

Prue frowned. "You think I don't know that? What do you think I've been doing all this time?"

Rachelle gave her a pained look. "I understand, but you can't go jumping off at the deep end because of a dream. Nikki will be worried if she notices you're upset."

Prue's thoughts were elsewhere. "If he does find us our lives, and not only Nikki's and mine, but his too, will be turned upside down. He'll want visitation rights and holiday time and…"

"Honey, stop." She motioned with her finger. "Bottoms up."

Prue shook her head. "I don't need alcohol I need a place to hide."

"What you need is to get on with your life and worry about Nicholas Colton if and when he shows up at your door."

Prue gave Rachelle a disgruntled sideward glance.

"It's the truth. Don't make waves where there are none." She swallowed the rest of her Bourbon.

Prue stood up and sat her glass on Rachelle's desk. "I know you mean well, but you're not in my position." She walked over to the door. "I'll see you in the studio."

Later that afternoon, Prue and Rachelle sat down to discuss the Halloween event they were attending. Because Rachelle had four VIP tickets they'd need to find escorts for the evening.

Prue's big brother, Toby, who was only three years older, had called during the day to say he would be in town on business from the twenty-seventh to the thirty-first of October, and asked if he could crash at her place. She was delighted he was coming to New York and more than happy to have him stay for a few days. She asked if he would be her date for the Halloween bash and he agreed. He said it would be a lot of fun and that he'd look forward to it.

Rachelle had organized a date for herself with a well-known anchorman so it was all set. "Halloween bash at the Maple, here we come!"

Prue had second thoughts about attending, but after some serious persuasion from her best friend she decided it would take her mind off the situation for a while. She needed the distraction.

Rachelle made the choice to go as the Black Widow from The Avengers movie, and her date had chosen a Captain America costume. They would look great together as a sexy crime-fighting duo.

Prue knew she wouldn't be able to talk her brother into wearing a Dr. Frank N Furter outfit, so she arranged a Brad costume for him instead, which consisted of a pair of spectacles, a white business shirt and a pair of gray pants. She knew he wouldn't be comfortable going in his underwear, even though he had a decent body.

As much as she'd had reservations about going out on Halloween, Prue realized it would be a lot of fun, especially with her brother accompanying her. She was glad he was coming to The Big Apple.

New York had fast become home for Prue and she hoped it would bring her some good fortune. She also hoped Nicholas Colton would remain in California and forget he ever met her.

Eleven

The days leading up to Halloween seemed to fly by and Prue was surprised when Toby knocked on her door at 8.00 p.m. on the night of the twenty-seventh. With everything going on in her life she'd lost track of time. He had driven the six hours from Pittsburgh to New York in his beat up, 1966 Mustang convertible. He adored her (Jessie) and planned to 'fix her up' one day.

Prue gave her big brother a huge hug and, unbeknown to him, a tear slid down her cheek. She was so happy to have him there. Nikki came flying out of her room the minute she heard his voice. "Uncle Toby!" she squealed and launched herself into his arms.

"Hey, baby girl, how are ya," he said, wrapping his arms around her in a tight bear hug.

She held up her index finger wrapped in a Band-Aid.

Toby frowned at it. "What happened?"

"Billy bit me."

"He did? Do you need me to sort him out for you?"

Nikki giggled. "Nah. I punched him in the arm so we're even."

Toby stood his niece on the floor. "Good for you. I bet he won't try that again."

"Please don't encourage her." Prue frowned at him.

Nikki gazed up at her mom. "Is Uncle Toby staying with us?"

"Yes, honey, remember I…" Prue realized not only had she lost track of time but she'd forgotten to tell her daughter about her uncle's visit. "Never mind, sweetie, mommy forgot. Yes, he's staying for a few days."

"Yay!" Nikki jumped up and down clapping her hands. "I love you Uncle Toby." She wrapped her arms around his thighs.

Toby bent down and touched the tip of her nose with his index finger. "I love you, too, Jellybean."

"Time to go back to bed, honey, you've got school tomorrow. You can talk to Uncle Toby in the morning." She took her daughter's hand and told her brother she wouldn't be long.

Toby kissed his niece goodnight then made himself

comfortable on the sofa. When Prue returned to the living room, her brother was stretched out, his feet hanging over the armrest, sound asleep. She wondered if she should wake him for something to eat. She crossed the room and shook his shoulder. "Tobe?" She shook him again. "Toby, are you hungry? Can I make you something?"

Her brother's eyes opened slowly. "Huh? Sorry sis, didn't mean to do that." He swung his long legs over the side of the sofa and sat up, rubbing his eyes. "Long drive." He chuckled. "What'd you say?"

Prue sat down beside him and slapped his thigh. "Can I make you something to eat?"

Toby yawned. "Yeah, that'd be great. Thanks. Don't go to too much trouble though. A grilled cheese sandwich will do just fine."

Prue got up off the sofa. "Grilled cheese it is." She headed to the kitchen to heat the skillet.

Her brother stood up, stretched his lean six foot two inch frame and followed her. "Settled in, ok? Like it here? Mom misses you, you know."

"Yeah, I know, we miss you all too, but I had to do this for me and Nikki."

Toby raised his hands. "Hey, you're preachin' to the converted here. I'm proud of you."

Prue gave a thin smile. "Thanks. I think we've settled in ok. Nikki's made some friends at her preschool and one little girl lives here in our building, which is great for her." She nodded. "Yeah, I do like it here."

Toby folded his arms and leaned against the doorframe. "As long as you're happy that's all that counts."

Prue gave a heavy sigh. "You're right."

"So what's up?" He could sense something was wrong.

"Nothing's up." Prue put on a happy face and attempted to hide her feelings. "Your grilled cheese will be ready in a couple minutes. Why don't you go make yourself comfortable at the table and I'll bring it in with a mug of coffee when it's done."

"Ok. Thanks." Toby watched her for a moment, then turned around and headed back into the living/dining room and sat down at the table. Drumming his fingers on the surface, he gazed around his sister's apartment. She had made the place comfortable for her and his niece.

Within minutes, Prue came into the room carrying a tray. She sat it on the dining table, handed Toby his grilled cheese sandwiches and set two mugs of coffee down. She slid the tray onto the server between the living room and kitchen and sat at the end of the table. "What's new with you, bro?"

"Bro?" His eyebrows rose and he grinned. "I'm thinking about selling the ranch," he told her, taking a bite of the gooey, toasted cheese sandwich.

Prue was surprised. "Why? I thought you loved it there. The rolling green acres, the fresh air, the horses. What happened?"

He sighed. "I do. But we haven't been turning a profit for a while. I had hoped things would pick up, but they haven't. It's the economy, I guess."

"I'm sorry to hear that. I hope something happens to keep it going." She rested a hand on his. "I love that place too." Although her brother was only thirty three, she noticed he looked much older these days. Maybe the stress of operating a failing business was taking its toll. She squeezed his hand. "Do what you have to, Tobe. It's not worth your health."

"That's why I'm in New York. I'm talking to a couple of investors to see if they'd be willing to inject some dollars into the ranch to build it up again. I've got two appointments this week. Fingers crossed, huh?"

"Absolutely. I wish I could help." She gazed at him with sad eyes.

Toby smiled. "I know. And I appreciate that." He frowned at her. "Wanna tell me what's really going on with you? I could always tell when you were unhappy about something. Still can."

Prue shifted her gaze from her brother to the blank television screen. She knew she couldn't look him in the face and say nothing was wrong. "I'm fine. Honestly."

"Wanna try that again looking at me this time?" He reached across, grabbed her chin gently and turned her face toward him. "What's wrong?"

"You didn't come here to listen to my troubles. You've got enough of your own. Everything's fine. I can handle it. Let's enjoy each other's company while you're here and have a fun night at the Halloween party on the weekend."

"Prudence." His frown deepened and he stared into her eyes.

"Don't try mom's trick. There's nothing to tell." As a teenager, whenever her mother looked her in the eye and called her Prudence she couldn't help but tell her the truth. Not so much these days, though.

"Hey, I'm concerned about you, that's all. What are big brothers for if their little sister can't cry on their shoulder once in a while?"

A sneaky tear slid down her cheek. Toby was on his feet pulling her into his arms and giving her a tight hug. "Tell your big brother what's wrong? I love you, sweetheart. I don't want to see you sad. Talk to me."

More tears spilled now. She sniffled and said, "If I start I might not be able to stop."

Toby walked her over to the sofa, sat her down and sat beside her. "I don't care if we're up all night. I'm here for you, you know that, right?"

Prue nodded and her chin quivered. She inhaled a deep breath to prevent herself from crying.

Toby got up, picked up the mugs of coffee and set them down on the coffee table, he also grabbed the tissues from off the server then took his seat. "You can start whenever you're ready. Ok?" He picked up his mug and swallowed a large mouthful of coffee. He was worried about her.

"Ok." Prue fidgeted with the tissue in her hand. Where would she begin?

Twelve

Prue told her big brother everything. How she'd met Nicholas Colton that night at Hemingway's Café, how they hadn't exchanged names. She regretted that now. She also told him how much she'd wanted to find him and tell him about Nikki but didn't know how. How she felt about him, despite her attempts to forget him. When she'd run into the author at Macy's she was afraid, after all this time, that if she told him he would be furious with her. And who knew what he might do?

Toby listened without interruption. He knew his little sister needed to get everything off her chest. He didn't judge her, it wasn't his place. After her fiancé, Connor, who was Toby's best friend, had been killed in a light plane crash at only twenty three, Toby didn't think Prue would ever recover. She had been shattered by her childhood sweetheart's death and it had taken a couple of years for her to pull herself out of the deep depression. Toby had had to be strong, despite the overwhelming grief he'd felt at the loss of his friend, to help his little sister through the heartbreak.

Once again, he wanted to be there to support her in any way he could. She needed it after everything she'd been through. Prue hadn't told her family the circumstances behind her pregnancy and now he understood why. Not that anyone would have judged her. They loved her and had watched her suffer the agony of losing the only man she had ever loved.

When she finished her story Toby wrapped his arms around her and gave her another one of those big bear hugs she loved so much. "I'm sorry you've had to go through this alone. You could've told me, you know."

Prue eased herself out of his arms. "I know, but I didn't want you to think any less of me for doing something so stupid." A tear slid down her cheek and she dabbed at it with the tissue.

"Hey, it's not stupid to want to be loved. And from what you've said he sounds like a decent guy who treated you well." He wrapped an arm around her shoulders and pulled her against him. "What are you going to do now?"

"I don't think it would be a good idea to disrupt his or our lives. He has a busy writing career and Nikki and I are just starting out here. What would be the good of telling him now?"

Toby lifted her face up to meet his gaze. "Because the man needs to know he has a child."

Prue sat up and frowned at her brother. "Does he? He should have taken responsibility that night so that something like this didn't happen." She regretted the words as soon as they left her mouth because it meant she wouldn't have Nikki, and she loved her daughter with all her heart.

Toby's eyebrows rose. "Do you think that's fair? You were both there."

Prue sighed. "Ok. Yes. You're right, we were. I – I don't know what I think, to be honest. One thing I do know is I don't want Nikki's life turned upside down. You can understand that, right?"

Her brother rubbed her back. "Of course I can. But he does have a right to know."

"Maybe. But not right now." She stood up. "Want more coffee?"

Toby handed her the mugs from off the coffee table. "Sure. Thanks." He could see his sister was conflicted about what to do and he didn't want to add any more pressure to her already confused state of mind.

The next morning, after another night of very little sleep, Prue set about making breakfast and packing lunch for her daughter. Toby was fast asleep on the sofa and Nikki was getting ready for the school day ahead, dressing in the clothes Prue had laid out for her and organizing her backpack. She was a great little helper in the morning.

Prue began setting the table as quietly as she could before having to wake her brother. He had driven several hours, and then spent most of the night listening to her woes before camping out on her uncomfortable sofa. Toby stirred and turned over. He was still in his clothes. "Hey, morning, sis."

"Good morning." Prue grimaced. "I didn't wake you, did I? I was trying to be quiet."

Toby stood up and stretched. "No, you didn't wake me. I've been lying here half-awake for a while." He walked over and took the plates and cutlery from her hands. "Let me do that. I need to earn my keep while I'm here." He grinned.

"Thanks. How does bacon and eggs sound?" She turned toward the server and sniffed. "I'd better go check on breakfast before it burns." She rushed into the kitchen.

"Sounds great," Toby called after her. "I'm starved." He finished setting the table.

Nikki brought her schoolbag into the hall and sat it by the door. "Morning, Uncle Toby." She ran over to him, threw her arms around his neck and planted a big kiss on his cheek as he bent down to pick her up.

"Good morning, Princess. Have a good sleep?" He tickled her neck and she giggled.

"Stop that!" She giggled more. "Yeah, I had a good sleep. Did you?"

"I sure did." He tossed her over his shoulder, carried her to the table and sat her on a chair.

Prue came into the room with two large plates – one containing fried eggs and the other piled high with bacon and toast. She glanced at the wall clock. "We'll have to hurry." She served an egg and some bacon to Nikki then passed the plate to her brother. "Do you have any appointments today?"

Toby shook his head. "Tomorrow and Thursday."

"Oh, ok. So are you staying here all day? Maybe catch up on some sleep?"

"I might do some sightseeing. Always wanted to visit the Statue of Liberty and the Empire State. If you like I can drive you and Nikki to preschool and then drop you at work. I can pick her up later too, if that's any help."

Prue smiled. "That'd be great." She squeezed his hand. "Thank you."

"Not a problem." He got stuck into his breakfast, scooping egg onto a slice of toast and taking a large bite.

"Yay!" Nikki said. "Wanna meet my teacher, Uncle Toby? Miss Foster. She's really nice."

"Maybe another time, Jellybean. Ok?"

Nikki pouted. "Ok," she droned.

Prue popped an egg and some bacon and toast onto her plate, but wasn't at all hungry. She sighed and cut into the egg, the yellow yoke running into the rashers of crispy bacon, but didn't lift it onto her fork.

Toby noticed. "You ok?"

She glanced over at him. "Yes, I'm ok. Just not hungry, that's all."

He rested a hand on her shoulder. "Things will work out. Trust that."

Prue gave him a thin smile. "I hope so."

"What's wrong, Mommy?" Nikki frowned.

Prue mustered her best smile. "Nothing, honey. Eat up we have to get going."

♥

After dropping Nikki at preschool, Toby drove his sister to the broadcast center. When he saw the huge complex he was awestruck. "Wow! That's some building. Almost takes up a whole city block."

"Yes, it's pretty impressive, huh?" Prue swung the door open and was about to get out when she saw Nicholas Colton stepping into the revolving door. "Oh, no!"

Toby gazed out the windshield of his Mustang. "What's wrong?"

Prue settled back in the seat and pulled the door closed. "It's him."

"The author?"

Prue nodded.

"Aren't you going to go talk to him?"

"No. He doesn't know I work here. At least I don't think he does." She frowned at the moving door. "I wonder why he's here."

"Maybe he's on the show," Toby surmised.

"He's already been on Rachelle's show. And she would've told me if she knew he was coming back in." Prue hoped Rachelle would, anyhow.

"Can you please take me home, Tobe? I'll call in sick today."

"If you're sure that's what you want."

She gave her brother an uncomfortable sideward glance, knowing he didn't approve. "Yes, it is. Thank you."

Thirteen

Trick-or-treating had been so much fun! New York knew how to turn on the spooky Halloween spirit. Toby had joined Prue and Yolanda, giving the kids turns at sitting on his broad shoulders when they ran out of steam from walking the few blocks. Nikki, Jazz and Sammy were giggling as they ran down the busy sidewalk with their stash of Halloween contraband, while the ladies strolled along arm in arm chatting not far behind them.

It was eight o'clock and had already been dark for a couple of hours. The buildings along the street were lit up with Jack O Lanterns, witches, ghost, goblins, ghouls, vampire bats and so much more. The group headed toward home, and Prue was glad she and her brother were going to the Halloween party later. She was in a good mood and looking forward to a night of adult fun.

By the time they arrived back at their apartment building, Nikki, Jazz and Sammy were ready to fall into bed, exhausted from the hours of running rampant trick-or-treating. Yolanda gathered them together and ushered them up the stairs, saying she had enjoyed the evening and telling Prue and Toby to have a fun time at the bash.

Prue thanked her for minding Nikki then unlocked her front door and stepped inside followed by Toby dressed as a cowboy. He owned several Stetsons and always had one in his car. Being a horse rancher, he never went anywhere without his hat.

She made a dash for the bathroom and then went into her room to freshen up her makeup before Rachelle came by to pick them up.

When she came back to the living room her brother was watching the TV. "Hey, Tobe, want something to eat or will you be ok till we get to the party?"

Toby lowered the volume and turned around. "Are you having something?"

Prue shook her head. "No, I think I'll wait."

"Ok then, me too." He turned the volume back up and continued watching the program.

She crossed the room and sat down beside him. "Are you planning on getting dressed soon?"

"Uh, yeah, in a bit," Toby said, tuned in to what was on the television.

The doorbell rang and Prue got up to answer it. She snuck a peek through the peephole before opening the door. Her nerves were always on edge every time the doorbell rang since she'd had that dream. Rachelle was early. "Hi, I thought you weren't coming over till nine thirty."

Rachelle sidled past Prue and into the entry hall. "I know, but I thought I'd stop by early so we can spend some time before we go."

Prue wondered what was on Rachelle's mind. "Is everything alright?"

"Everything's great. So looking forward to tonight, it's going to be a blast."

Toby turned off the television and stood up.

Prue introduced him. "This is my brother Toby. Tobe, this is Rachelle Reed."

He walked over and shook her hand. "Good to meet you, Rachelle. I've seen your show a couple times."

"Thanks. Nice to meet you too." Rachelle couldn't take her eyes off him. He was a tall, attractive cowboy.

"Sis, can I use your room to get changed?" Toby asked, gathering up the pieces of his costume.

"Of course you can." She motioned down the hallway. "You know where it is."

Toby disappeared into Prue's room, closing the door behind him.

"So that's your brother, huh?"

"Yep, that's him. Don't get any ideas, either. He's spoken for." Not that he was right now, but Rachelle didn't need to know that.

Her friend's face dropped. "That's a pity. Sexy much."

"Rachelle!"

"He's a looker. And let's face it there aren't many *real men* left in the world today."

Prue glowered at her. "Have you forgotten he's my brother?" She didn't need to hear Rachelle's thoughts on how sexy Toby was.

"Oh. Yeah. Sorry."

Toby came back along the hall in his Brad costume minus the pants. Prue was taken aback when he walked into the living room. He looked like the real Brad in the scene in Frank's laboratory. Rachelle couldn't take her eyes off his long athletic legs and Prue nudged her.

"What happened to the pants?" Prue asked.

"I've seen the movie. Brad doesn't have any pants in

the mansion and as I have all the components, oh, and these," he said, putting on the glasses, "I thought I'd go traditional Brad." His smile widened.

"Are you sure you'll be comfortable dressed that way?" Prue would have purchased the Dr. Frank N Furter costume if she'd known her brother was an exhibitionist.

"Yeah, it's nothing. We're going to have some fun tonight, right?" He gave Rachelle a sideward glance.

Prue shook her head. He was acting like a rooster in a henhouse. Showoff.

☙ ♥ ❧

The Maple was cram-packed with characters from the movies: horror, superhero, action, sci fi and more. The group threaded their way through the dancing throng to the bar, and on the way they passed three Dracula, two Elvira, The Hulk, a couple of Bettie Boop, a zombie or two, three Captain Jack Sparrow, Sandy and Danny from Grease, and only one Dr. Frank N Furter (Prue was pleased she hadn't chosen that costume for Toby, after all), who shimmied when Prue passed him and gave her a seductive wink while licking his glossy red lips.

Prue blushed as she passed a celebrity couple she recognized dressed as Morticia and Gomez Addams. She had no idea some of the rich and famous would attend the party and was excited to be there. Then again, Rachelle was a celebrity in her own right. She noticed a couple more well-known celebs as she followed Rachelle through the crowd and Rachelle stopped to say hello. Introductions all round, not that anyone could hear, then on to the bar for a drink. The Maple had a one hour complimentary Vodka open bar and they had already missed the first half hour.

The live DJ was rocking the house with a medley of Top 40 hits, hip hop, and mash ups.

The TV host knew the guy behind the counter and pre-ordered drinks for throughout the evening so they wouldn't have to wait. The perks of being famous.

While Rachelle waited for their drinks, Toby and Prue gazed around the lounge looking for a place to sit. Everywhere was taken.

With drinks in hand, they made their way back through the throng of revelers and out to the street. Tom would arrive at any minute and Rachelle wanted to be situated somewhere he could find her. She held up her drink. "Happy Halloween."

Rachelle's date arrived fifteen minutes later dressed in his Captain America costume and took her breath away. "God, you look gorgeous! I want to eat you up right now."

"You look pretty gorgeous yourself." He leaned in to kiss her cheek and whispered something in her ear. Rachelle giggled and play slapped him. "You're wicked."

She introduced Prue and Toby to Tom and handed him a drink that she'd brought down with her. One she had considered drinking if he hadn't arrived when he did.

Maple staff was collecting empty glasses and the group handed them theirs before heading back inside to get some boogie on. Rachelle danced her way through the party goers, her hands in the air. Tom caught up to her and slid his arms around her waist forming a mini conga line. Prue and her brother danced behind them following them through the crowd.

After a couple of hours of dancing, the DJ took a well-earned break and Rachelle headed to the bar for more drinks. When she reached the counter a voice behind her caught her off guard and she swung around.

"Hi, Rachelle. Great bash, huh?" Nicholas Colton looked gorgeous dressed as The Mad Hatter from Tim Burton's adaptation of Alice in Wonderland.

"Hello, yourself. Yes, it is. What are you doing here?" She glanced past him to see if she could pick out Prue in the masses.

"My publisher invited me. She's here somewhere."

He glanced over his shoulder. "Haven't seen the wicked Queen from Snow White and the Huntsman by any chance?"

"Sorry, no. Been here long?" Her eyes continued to search for Prue and Toby. If she spotted his lanky frame, she'd find her friend.

"Only ten minutes or so. Are you here with people?" He looked around her.

"Yes. Not sure where my entourage is at the moment though." She gave him a big smile. "Well, I'd better get these drinks back to the thirsty, wherever they are. Have fun. Hope you find your publisher."

"Thanks. Hope you find your entourage." He grinned.

"Me too." She threaded through the crowd as fast as she could, looking for Prue. *Where did they go?*

Rachelle's heart was doing the rumba and it had nothing to do with the music. If Nicholas spotted Prue the whole thing was over. *Maybe they went back outside.* She made her way to the front entrance. When she stepped out into the cool, New York evening she shivered and wasn't sure if it was the night air or her nerves that caused her body to react that way.

Her three friends were standing off to the right, so Rachelle weaved her way through the Halloween revelers on the sidewalk and rushed over to them, handing the drinks around and pulling Prue to one side. "Nicholas is here."

"What?! Where?" Prue's eyes darted around the costume-clad crowd milling on the street.

"Inside. I spoke to him at the bar. He said his publisher invited him. Do you want to leave before he sees you?"

"I don't think he'd recognize me in this costume, do you? And if he's looking for his publisher maybe he'll stay inside."

"I don't know, your face still looks the same, hon. I hope he does stay inside for your sake."

The two women joined the men.

Toby leaned in to his sister and spoke into her ear. "Everything ok?"

Prue rested her hand on his arm and kissed his cheek. "Nothing to worry about, big brother. Promise."

Nicholas stepped out of the Maple and spotted the group of four standing near the railing. He immediately recognized the woman he had spent the night with in Pittsburgh. He couldn't mistake that beautiful face even in the bright red wig and sparkly gold hat. She was kissing the man standing beside her. The man she had been with in

LA when they had run into each other at Macy's department store. He had the sudden urge to rush over there, take her in his arms and kiss her, but as much as he wanted to he couldn't disrupt her life.

Missed chances. Would the timing ever be right for them? He couldn't get her out of his head or his heart so what was he to do now?

Fourteen

Early Monday morning, Nicholas traveled by cab to the broadcast center. He was certain the TV host knew who the woman was that he had met in Pittsburgh, and he hoped she would help him. He entered the CBS foyer and walked over to the front desk. "Good morning. Is it possible to speak to Rachelle Reed please?"

The young woman behind the counter smiled up at him. "Good morning, Mr. Colton. Let me check for you." She telephoned Rachelle's office. No answer. She disconnected the call and turned to the author. "I'm sorry Mr. Colton Rachelle doesn't seem to be here yet."

"Nicholas sighed. "Ok. Can I leave her a message?"

"Of course." She passed him a notepad and pen.

The author wrote down his details and asked Rachelle to contact him as soon as possible, then tore off the page, folded it and handed it to the receptionist. "Would you please make sure she gets this as soon as she comes in? It's very important."

"Absolutely. I'll hand it to her myself." She placed the note in an envelope, sealed it and wrote Rachelle's name on the front.

"Thank you. I'd appreciate that." Nicholas hesitated before leaving. Maybe he should wait for the TV host to arrive. No, that would appear desperate. He headed for the door. Was he doing the right thing? *'All's fair in love and war'* popped into his head. He shook the thought from his mind, shuffled through the revolving door and stepped onto the street.

"Taxi." He hailed a cab heading in the opposite direction and moved onto the road. The driver did a U-turn and pulled up in front of him. Nicholas opened the door, then turned and glanced at the broadcast center before getting in, wondering if he should have waited. He hoped Rachelle would contact him soon. As the taxi pulled away Nicholas spotted her getting out of another cab. "Stop the car!" He needed to speak to her face to face, needed to find out who the woman was that he'd made passionate love to all those years ago. Needed the chance to tell her how he felt. He handed the driver a couple of large bills for the inconvenience and threw the door open. "Rachelle," he called, hurrying toward her.

The TV host turned around and her eyes widened. *Why is he here?* She put on her best smile and walked over to him. "Well, hello again. What brings you here?"

Nicholas' expression was serious. "I need to talk to you about a personal matter. Can we speak in your office?"

Rachelle's heartbeat ticked up a notch and she couldn't take a breath for a second. "Personal? What do you mean?" She gave him an uncertain frown.

"I would prefer to discuss it somewhere private, if you don't mind?"

"Alright."

The pair headed into the building.

When they reached Rachelle's office, she closed the door and offered Nicholas a seat. She moved around her desk, sat down and asked him if he would like some coffee before he began. He declined.

"You said you wanted to discuss something personal. I'm not sure I understand how I can help." Rachelle clasped her hands on the desk in front of her.

"Saturday night at the Halloween party I saw you with a group of people standing outside the restaurant."

Oh, God, he knows!

"Go on." She attempted a smile to cover her nervous demeanor. This would mean Prue's dream *had* come true.

"I knew the woman dressed as Columbia a long time ago and I'd like to get in touch with her while I'm here. Can you help me do that?" Nicholas wasn't about to tell Rachelle he didn't know the woman's name.

"What makes you think I know her?"

"Body language mostly. People who know each other act in certain ways around one another. And your group looked intimate."

Rachelle shifted uncomfortably in her chair. "Really?"

"Oh, yes, as an author I've had to study body language to create authenticity in my novels." He crossed one leg over the other, leaned his elbows on the armrest and clasped his hands.

"Fascinating. But my date and I met the other couple there. I'm sorry I can't help you."

Nicholas could feel his patience dissolve. "Can't or won't?"

Rachelle popped up out of her chair. "If I could help you I would, but I can't." She smiled. "Is there anything else you need while you're in New York?"

Nicholas sighed and stood up. "No, thank you. If you do happen to see the woman again would you please give her my details? It's important that I reach her."

The TV host remained poker-faced. "I can't promise you that because I don't expect to see her again."

The author walked to the door and opened it. "Well, thanks for your time."

"Good seeing you again. Look forward to your next book." Once he'd left her office, Rachelle let out the breath she'd been holding and sank into her chair. She needed a minute before calling Prue.

Nicholas walked along the corridor wondering how he would ever get in touch with the woman. He knew Rachelle Reed hadn't been honest with him, that she knew more than she was telling. Body language told him that.

The TV host felt a pang of guilt for lying to the author, but Prue was her best friend and she wouldn't betray her trust, even though she believed Nicholas Colton had a right to know he had a child. She sat gazing out of the windowed wall to her office contemplating how to tell Prue he'd been there when she appeared in the doorway. She was early.

"Morning." Prue entered the office and sat in the chair occupied by the author only thirty minutes before.

"Morning, hon." Rachelle stood up, walked around the desk and leaned against the corner. "I have something to tell you."

Prue gave her a concerned frown. "What is it?"

Rachelle folded her arms. "Nicholas was here a half hour ago asking about you."

"What?" Prue popped up out of the chair. "What did you tell him?"

"He asked for your contact details. He'd seen us outside the Maple Saturday night and recognized you right away. He said it was important that he speaks to you. I told him we met at the party and that I didn't know you personally." She took her friend's hand and squeezed it. "What are you going to do?"

"I'm not sure." She sighed. "If he doesn't know that I work here..."

"Yes, but what if he finds out?" Rachelle returned to her chair.

Prue sat down. "He was here last week. Did you know about that?"

Rachelle's left eyebrow rose. "No. Do you know why?"

She shook her head. "I thought you might. I meant to ask you before now, but I've had a lot on my mind lately."

"I'll check." Rachelle picked up the cordless phone. "Hi Trace, can you tell me why Nicholas Colton was here last week? Oh. Uh-huh. Thanks. I appreciate it." She stood the phone on its base. "Apparently he came by to see if he could get a copy of the interview. Sounds logical, I guess."

"You don't think he was asking questions about me, do you?" Prue bit her bottom lip.

Rachelle shrugged. "I don't know, hon. Maybe."

Prue gave a huge sigh. "Did he leave a number?"

The TV host's eyebrows rose. "You're not thinking of calling him, are you?" She opened the top drawer, took out the note he had left and handed it to her friend.

She opened it and stared at the words written in black pen. "He has nice handwriting."

"Is that all you can say? I'm having kittens thinking about what could happen if he finds out where you are. What about Nikki?"

Prue's head shot up and she looked Rachelle in the eyes. "I don't know. And no, I'm not planning to call him. Not right away, anyhow. Maybe not at all."

Gabe appeared at the door. "Showtime, ladies."

Rachelle scowled at him. "You know what I'm going to say, don't you?"

"Go away?"

"Exactly." She pointed for him to leave.

"Biatch."

"Queen."

Prue stood up. "Stop it. Both of you!" She walked over to Gabe and rested a hand on his arm. "We'll be right there."

"At least you have some class, lovely." Gabe evil-eyed Rachelle then turned on his heel and marched down the corridor.

Prue frowned at her friend. "You shouldn't have said that."

"Well he shouldn't call be a bitch. Serves him right." She stood up and came around the desk.

"Not nice, Rachelle."

Rachelle looped her arm through Prue's. "So what are you going to do about Nicholas?"

"His book tour finishes at the end of next week so hopefully he'll fly back to California."

"You've been keeping track, huh?"

"Of course I have. I don't need any more surprises. There have been too many already, and today topped them all. Once he goes home and gets back into writing his next New York Times bestseller he'll forget all about me." At least she hoped he would.

Fifteen

Nicholas Colton sat in the passenger lounge at JFK Airport waiting for his flight to Monterey, his heart heavy. By now he had hoped to know more about the lovely woman he had lost his heart to. At least her name. Rachelle Reed knew more than she was letting on and he wondered why she wouldn't help him. His gut told him the TV host knew who the woman was, that, perhaps, they were friends and she was protecting her. But why? All he wanted to do was talk to her.

At 2.50 p.m. the boarding call for his flight was announced and Nicholas joined the queue of passengers waiting to embark. Something in the pit of his stomach told him he should stay, but he had no choice he had to leave. He was three quarters of the way into writing his next novel and on a strict deadline. His publisher wanted the manuscript on her desk by November 30. Not much time at all.

How would he concentrate on his work when he couldn't get his mind off the woman he'd made love to all those years ago? After seeing her again she was all he could think about.

The flight would take over five hours, so he decided to utilize the time writing. He had his laptop with him and it would be a good opportunity to work on the book while he was in the air. And, hopefully, take his mind off her for a while, although he didn't think that was possible.

Once the plane was at cruising altitude, Nicholas retrieved his MacBook from the overhead compartment, sat it on his lap and booted it up. No one occupied the seat next to him, so he could work without the possibility of interruption or prying eyes. He opened up the word document: *The Kill Game by Nicholas Colton word count: 61,528*. He was happy with the title and knew it was a perfect fit for the plot.

The five and a half hour flight flew by as he tapped away at the keyboard, and by the time they were ready to land he'd managed to get a few thousand words added to his word count, despite the woman's face hovering in the back of his mind. How could he find her?

One of his closest friends was a private investigator whose expertise was surveillance investigations, and Nicholas often picked his brain for plot ideas and correct protocol. Should he pick his brain about ways of finding the woman? Should he hire him to find her?

The announcement from the cockpit that the plane was five minutes out of Monterey Airport came over the PA system and Nicholas packed away his laptop and fastened his seatbelt. His friend would be picking him up from the airport, so he might broach the topic with him on the drive home.

❧♥❧

Prue was feeling blue. She missed her big brother and so did Nikki. It had been wonderful having him stay with them Halloween week, and now that he was gone the apartment felt different somehow. Everything had begun to feel different.

That afternoon, Prue had left work early to pick up her daughter from preschool so they could spend some mother daughter time together before bed. She had also ordered Chinese takeaway, something she didn't do often. It would be a nice treat for them both.

The doorbell rang and Nikki was excited about

having food delivered. She ran to the door and waited for her mom to open it. The young Asian guy told Prue the cost was $50.00 plus delivery. Prue paid him, including a tip, took the bag of aromatic cuisine and closed the door. Nikki bounced up and down like a Jack-in-the-Box. "It smells yummy, Mommy."

"Yes it does, can't wait to try it, can you?"

"Nope, I'm starving."

Prue carried the bag over to the table, pulled out a chair for her daughter then sat at the end and unpacked their dinner. She had already set their places in anticipation of the food arriving. She opened each container and sniffed the wonderful aroma. She had chosen three dishes including fried rice and a dessert.

While they ate, Nikki chattered away about school and her friends and what they did in class that day and Prue enjoyed every second of it. Her daughter also told her about one little boy named Paul, who only had a daddy because his mommy had gone to heaven. And then the unthinkable happened. "Mommy, where's my daddy?"

Prue's mouthful of food lodged in her throat and she swallowed hard to push the wad of gluey rice down into her stomach. She knew this day would come but she had hoped it wouldn't be for a couple of years... or more. She cleared her throat and wiped her mouth on a paper napkin. "Well, he – he's…"

The telephone rang and Prue left the table to answer it, breathing a sigh of relief. "Hello?"

"Hey, sis, it's me," Toby said.

"Hi, Tobe, what's up?" She was glad for the interruption. At least she wouldn't have to answer Nikki's question right away.

"I have to come back to New York for a couple days. I think one of the investors wants to negotiate a deal."

"That's wonderful news." Prue was pleased for her brother and happy he was coming back.

"Yeah, I think so. Anyhow, I was wondering…"

"Of course you can stay. This time you can have Nikki's room and she can bunk with me. I don't know why I didn't think of it before. I'm sorry you had to sleep on my uncomfortable sofa for so long."

"Hey, I didn't mind. It was great being there with you and Nikki. Please don't go to any trouble on my account, I'm not there to disrupt your life. The sofa's fine."

"No way, bro." Prue was adamant. "You're sleeping in your niece's room. No argument."

"Ok. You won't get any argument from me. I'll take what I can get." He chuckled.

"Good." Prue went quiet.

"Everything ok?"

She took the phone and walked down the hallway to her room. "Nikki asked me where her daddy is."

"And what did you tell her?"

"You called and saved my life once again. I didn't know what to say. I hope she's forgotten about it by the time I get off the phone."

"Don't count on it. When kids what answers they're like elephants, they don't forget."

"What am I supposed to say? I'm not prepared for this." Prue paced.

Toby thought for a moment. "Why don't you tell her he's away working? It's not far from the truth."

"What if she asks when he'll be back? Or what if she wants to see a picture of him?"

"Tell her there wasn't time to take a picture. He had to leave in a hurry and he'll let you know when he's finished working and on his way home."

Prue sighed. "And you think that's going to work?"

"She's only five. It should satisfy her curiosity for a while, until you can come up with something else."

"I guess you're right. Thanks, Tobe. What would I do without you?"

"Let's hope you never have to find out. Hey, I'll be in New York Sunday to Wednesday at this stage. Think you can put up with me for that long?" He chuckled.

"No different to last time. I know you've only been gone three weeks, but we've missed you."

"Aw, shucks, I missed you too. See you Sunday. Go talk to your daughter."

"Ok. See you then. Love you."

"Love ya too, sis." He rang off.

Prue walked back to the kitchen and hung up the phone. She wasn't ready to talk to Nikki about a daddy neither of them knew. But she had to tell her daughter something and Toby's idea was all she had. She hoped it was enough.

Sixteen

Once Rachelle's shows were recorded back to back she and Prue headed up to her office. It was Friday, at long last, and the TV host wanted to ask her friend if they could do more Christmas shopping on the weekend, in New York this time. She had some last minute things to pick up before she began the task of gift wrapping. When Prue told her Toby was coming to town again Rachelle's ears pricked up.

"How long will he be here?" She sat down behind her desk, kicked off stilettoes and rubbed her aching feet.

"Don't get any ideas. Like I said, he's spoken for." Prue plonked herself down in the chair in front of the desk. "Why are you so interested in him anyway?"

"Because he's a real man."

Prue chuckled. "You think so, huh?"

"Sure do. Is he really taken?" She grimaced.

"He's off limits."

Rachelle scowled at her. "But why? Can't I have a little fun with a cowboy? He's so sexy in his Stetson. He could leave that on."

"He's my *brother*. I don't want that kind of image stuck in my brain, thank you very much."

Her friend shrugged. "Don't think about it. Can't I ask him out for a drink?"

"No. You don't like him you've got the hots for him, there's a difference. What happened to Tony?"

"Tom. He was eye candy for the party. We didn't do anything."

"Oh, puhleeze, you were all over each other like a rash."

Rachelle crossed her heart with a well-manicured and polished fingernail. "I give you my word."

Prue waved it off. "Your word? Come on. I know you, remember?"

The TV host looked sheepish.

"Ha, I knew it!" Prue pointed at her. "Then it's a double *NO*. You keep your hands off my brother. He's a sweetheart and deserves someone who'll love him."

"Oh, alright, if I must. You're lucky I like you."

"You like me because I'm honest with you. You're a nice person most of the time, but you're a floozy."

Rachelle gave Prue a disgruntled frown. "Not entirely. I prefer a smorgasbord not the same course over and over. Is there anything wrong with that? Men can do it and no one bats an eyelid. Why can't women? It is the twenty-first century, after all."

Prue sighed. "Ok. Don't say I didn't warn you. You wouldn't want all the men you go out with to fall for you at the same time, would you?"

Her friend scoffed. "That will never happen. And I'm only seeing three."

"I'm serious about Toby."

"Such a waste." Rachelle gave a heavy sigh and decided to take her mind off him by changing the subject. "Has Nikki asked anymore questions about her daddy?"

"No, thank goodness. She seems to be ok with the fact that he's away working, at least for now."

"So what are you going to say if she does ask?"

"I'll stay with the story I've already told her."

Rachelle leaned on the desk. "That's not going to satisfy her curiosity forever. She'll want answers one day. Real ones. What then?"

"Not for a long time I hope. I'll work it out by then."

"Have you given any more thought to calling Nicholas? You kept his note, didn't you?"

"Yes, I have it. But I still maintain that it wouldn't be fair to disrupt our life or his. Things have been fine so far. Why change it?"

"Because your daughter is asking questions. I think that's a pretty good reason."

Prue folded her arms. "Let's get through the holidays first, then maybe I'll think about it."

"Ok." Rachelle clapped her hands together. "So are we shopping Saturday?"

"Sure. I still haven't bought my dad a gift yet and I want to get some stocking stuffers too."

"Great. I'll pick you up around 8.00. It'll give us time for a coffee before we get into some serious shopping. Only five weeks to go, you know."

"I know. Nikki's so excited that Santa will be here soon. And I'm really looking forward to going home."

"It'll be nice for you. I'm heading home too."

"That's great. Take lots of photos. I'd love to see pics of your family."

"Speaking of family, I need to pick up a new pair of leather boots for my mom. She's been dropping hints about them for ages so I thought I'd make them one of her

Christmas gifts. I saw the pair she likes in Macy's online catalog and thought we could check them out while we're shopping."

Prue's body tightened at the mention of the department store. "At least I won't run into Nicholas here. That's a plus."

"Don't put it out there, hon."

Prue pressed her lips together and pulled an imaginary zipper across her mouth. Rachelle was right. *Don't* put it out there.

Seventeen

Nicholas Colton was at his desk in his home office working on the final revision for his next novel, *The Kill Game,* before express posting a copy off to his publisher. She was of the old school and preferred to read a hard copy to an electronic file. He was also of the old school and always typed THE END when he finished a book, much to her chagrin. Some of the classic authors did it and he was enamored with writers such as Agatha Christie and Ernest Hemingway. Nicholas hoped to write a literary classic one day.

He gazed out of the panoramic window. The view was spectacular overlooking the cliffs: Cypress trees swaying in the autumn breeze, foamy turquoise waves rolling to shore, and the clear, pale blue sky were perfect. He leaned back in his comfortable office chair, took off his glasses and rubbed his eyes, he was glad the book was finished. It had been a difficult task because he couldn't get the woman he'd met all those years ago and again only weeks ago out of his mind. She had lived in his heart for so long how could he move on without telling her?

His faithful canine buddies Rocky and Benji stirred. They'd been lying at his feet the whole afternoon. It was time to take them for a well-earned walk.

Nicholas stood up and stretched. He was a little stiff from sitting so long. When he glanced at the computer's digital time he was surprised to see it was almost five o'clock. "Come on, fellas, let's go for that walk." The Rottweilers were on their feet, tongues out, tails wagging.

While the author walked the coastline with his dogs, he wondered about the woman he was so desperate to find. Where did she live? Who was the man he'd seen her with at the Halloween party? Was she married? Peter, his PI friend, said he'd do some digging but couldn't promise much without anything to go on. Nicholas was grateful for his help but knew he was right. It was a dead end without a name.

He walked down to the beach and let his dogs off their leashes so they could run along the sand and splash in the water. He sat on the rocks watching them frolic in the surf. They were good company while he worked. Writing was a solitary occupation, but something he loved to do. He'd been a lawyer back in the day and made a comfortable living, but even though he helped people it didn't fulfil him and he knew he had to pursue his dream. The emotional ordeal of losing his wife made him realize that life was indeed too short, so he handed in his resignation, started writing and never looked back.

The alarm went off on his Apple Watch and he called the dogs in. He clipped on their leashes and headed back to the house. When he reached the porch his PI friend, Peter Moncrieff and a guy he didn't know were waiting for him. "Hey, good to see you." Nicholas shook his friend's hand. "Want some coffee?"

"I thought you'd never ask. It's chilly up here with the sea air drifting in." He introduced the guy standing next to him. "This is Colin Lang. He's a sketch artist for the city's police department. I thought maybe you could describe the woman you're looking for and see what he can come up with."

Nicholas shook Colin's hand. "I appreciate your time. Thanks." He unlocked the front door. "Come on in the coffee's already brewed."

The three men entered the house and headed to the

galley style kitchen. Nicholas poured three mugs of coffee and they sat down at the breakfast table. Colin took a large sketch pad out of his rucksack and sat it in front of him along with a couple of thick lead pencils and an eraser.

"What do you need to know?" Nicholas asked.

Colin peeled back the cover and picked up a pencil. "Start with the basic facial features first and we'll go from there."

"Ok. Uh, her face is kind of heart-shaped. Her cheekbones are high and… and she has a small dimple in her chin."

Colin started to sketch. "That's good. I'll get you to go into more detail in a minute."

"Sure." Nicholas took a sip of his coffee and glanced at Peter.

"Colin's good at what he does. He should be able to recreate the woman's face from your description down to the last detail."

Nicholas' heart thudded against his ribs. At last he'd have something to go on. A picture paints a thousand words, and someone, somewhere, knew who she was. He was going to find her.

Two hours later, Peter left the pair to call for pizza delivery. It was getting late and none of them had eaten.

Nicholas and Colin were working well together and he knew his colleague would have an accurate facial composite of the woman by the time he finished. She must have been someone special for his friend to want to find her so badly. Nicholas hadn't been interested in anyone since Pamela died so if this mystery woman could bring him some happiness that's all that mattered.

By ten o'clock the sketch was complete. Nicholas stared at the beautiful face on the sheet of paper and gave a happy sigh. It was her.

❧ ♥ ❧

Prue sat on the sofa, her MacBook on her lap, sifting through memories: photos of her family, Nikki when she was a baby, and her fiancé, Connor Bennett. When he died she thought she would never be able to feel again, let alone love again. They had grown up together, childhood sweethearts, and he had been her whole world.

When he'd proposed to her on their fifth anniversary as a couple she had known in her heart of hearts that he was the one. They had waited to become engaged because Connor wanted to build a house for them before they were married. Their dream home stood unfinished on the block of land they had bought together, not far from her brother's horse ranch, and she couldn't bear to go near it. She had thought about selling, but it was all she had left of their life together, and she wasn't sure she'd ever be ready to let it go.

Prue gave a heavy sigh and clicked on a baby photo of her daughter. What did Nicholas look like when he was a baby? How much did Nikki resemble him? She'd never given it any thought until that moment. If he did ever meet their little girl would he know she was his?

She sat her laptop on the coffee table and walked down the hallway to her daughter's room, cracked the door open and peered inside. Nikki was fast asleep hugging her favorite teddy bear. She loved her so much and that was the reason why she wanted to keep Nicholas Colton at a distance. It would be too much of a disruption bringing him into their lives after so many years. Her brother's words echoed in her head, 'The man has a right to know he has a child.' Prue closed the door and walked back along the hall.

She felt guilty for wanting to be selfish and protect her daughter. Who knew if the man wanted to know? Everyone assumed he did, but what if he didn't? He was a celebrity author. Wouldn't a child cramp his jetsetter lifestyle?

Rachelle had said he was a nice man, but how nice would he be if he found out he had a child he never knew about? A child who was five years old? Things could get ugly: a custody battle and shared visitation rights. Prue shivered at the thought. She didn't want that for her happy, well-adjusted little girl.

A knock on her front door made her jump. *Who could that be at this late hour?* It was ten o'clock. She stepped up to the peephole and peered through it, her stomach flipping over when she saw the dark hair.

Her breath caught in her throat and she stepped backwards.

Another three raps.

"Hey, sis, are you going to let me in or do I have to sleep outside your door all night?"

Toby!

She slid back the security chain, unlocked the deadlock and threw open the door. "Hi. Didn't you say tomorrow? It was meant to be Sunday, right?"

"Yeah, but I thought I'd surprise you, seeing as you missed me and all." His smile broadened.

Prue gave him a huge hug. "I'm so glad you're here." She picked up the bag at his feet. "Come on in. Hungry?"

"You bet."

"Nikki's asleep. Do you mind sleeping on the sofa tonight?"

"Nope. Not at all." He took the bag from Prue and set it down in the hallway beside the front door. "It's good to be out of the car. I don't care where I crash."

"What do you feel like eating?" she asked, heading into the kitchen.

Her brother followed. "Same as before will do fine."

"I've got some leftover lasagna if you'd prefer that. It won't take long to heat in the microwave."

"That'd be great. I'll go wash up while you do what you're doing. Be right back." He headed down the hall to the bathroom.

Prue popped the lasagna into the microwave, then went into the living room and closed her laptop. She didn't want to get into a discussion about Connor or Nicholas tonight.

Prue drifted into a restless dream after lying in bed unable to sleep for over two hours. She tossed and turned and rolled onto her back, her breathing shallow.

Nicholas was there.

Prue could feel his gentle hands caressing her, his warm breath on her skin as his lips moved from her mouth, down her throat and across her shoulder. His mouth trailed slow kisses down her stomach to the place she longed for him to taste…

Prue gasped awake, her heart racing. She sprang up in bed and gazed around the shadows of her room. *Nicholas?*

It was a dream.

Had she moaned out loud? She hoped not. Her brother was sleeping only a short distance down the hall.

Prue flopped back onto the pillow with a frustrated huff… unsatisfied, tears stinging the backs of her eyes. She didn't want to admit to herself that she longed to have Nicholas in her bed making love to her again, despite her fear of what could happen if she allowed him into her life.

Eighteen

Early Sunday morning, Nikki peeked into her mom's room and saw she was still asleep. Not wanting to wake her up, Nikki thought she would try to make breakfast for herself. She headed to the kitchen and frowned at the bag sitting in the hallway. When she realized whose it was, she raced across the living room, launched herself into the air and landed on top of her uncle.

Toby woke with a jolt, expelling a large whoosh of air from his mouth.

"Uncle Toby, you're here!" she exclaimed shrilly, leaning in and planting a firm kiss on his forehead.

"Hey, Jellybean, where's your mom?" He yawned and peered over his head into the kitchen. Prue wasn't there.

Nikki raised her index finger to her lips and lowered her voice. "She's still sleeping. Can you please make me breakfast?"

Toby lifted his niece onto the floor and sat up. "Sure can. What'll it be?"

The little girl ran to the kitchen, took a bowl out of the cupboard under the counter and placed it carefully on top. Her uncle followed. "I'm allowed Lucky Charms on the weekend. I *love* them." She pointed to an overhead cupboard. "They're in there."

Toby took out the box of colorful cereal, poured some into the bowl and added milk. He found the cutlery drawer and grabbed a spoon, then took the bowl into the dining room and sat it on the table. "There ya go."

Nikki pulled out the chair and climbed up. "Thank you, Uncle Toby."

"You're welcome, little lady. Eat up while I go make the coffee."

Prue emerged from her bedroom ten minutes later to the pungent, nutty aroma of freshly brewed coffee. It smelled so good and she needed the caffeine hit to get the day started. She peeked into the living/dining room and saw her brother and her daughter having breakfast together. "Morning. Sorry I slept in."

Toby glanced over at her and smiled. "No problem. We managed."

"Coffee smells good." She closed her eyes, breathed in the wonderful aroma and sighed.

"Here, why don't you sit and I'll get you a cup." Toby got up from the table and walked over to her.

Prue looked up at her tall brother and smiled. "Thanks." She wandered over to the table, sat down next to Nikki and gave her a hug and a kiss. "Mommy's sorry she slept in, honey. Love you."

Nikki patted her mom's face. "That's ok, Mommy. Uncle Toby made me breakfast."

Toby sat the mug of coffee in front of Prue and went back to his seat. "How'd you sleep? Manage to get any?"

"Not much. I'm looking forward to coming home for the holidays. It'll be good to be with family for a while, and I could use the break."

"It'll be great having you home. Why don't I drive in, spend the night and we can head back Christmas Eve morning?" Toby said.

Prue's eyebrows rose. "You want to drive all this way to pick us up? No. We can take the bus, it's fine."

"You'll have cases and presents and food. It'll be easier and safer if I come get you."

"Tobe, I appreciate that, but it's such a long way."

"I don't mind. So it's settled then. I'll be here on the afternoon of the twenty-third and we'll leave bright and early on the twenty-fourth so we'll be home in plenty of time for dinner. Mom's got something special planned."

Prue smiled. "Ok. I'd really like that." She reached across the table and gave her brother's hand a squeeze. "Thank you."

"No thanks required." He grinned and sipped his coffee.

"I can't wait to see grandma and grandpa," Nikki said. "I miss them."

"Well they miss you too, Princess," her uncle said. "Grandma's got something special for you too."

Nikki beamed. "She has?"

"Yep, she sure does."

The little girl turned to her mom, excited. "How long till Christmas, Mommy?"

"Let me see." She calculated in her head. "About twenty-five sleeps, give or take. Not long now."

"Yay!" Nikki clapped her hands, a huge smile spreading across her face. "I can't wait to see what Santa brings me. Maybe daddy will be home by then too."

Prue and Toby's eyes met. That was unexpected. It

was obvious to Prue that Nikki was still thinking about him. She also realized it would only intensify as time moved on.

"Maybe he will, honey." Prue put on her best smile for her daughter.

"Can I go play now, please?"

"Of course, sweetie."

Nikki jumped off the chair, took her bowl to the kitchen, then ran down the hallway to her room.

Prue sighed. "That totally threw me. She must be wondering about him more than I thought."

"Looks that way. What are you going to do?"

"Honestly? I have no idea. But I'll have to think of something."

Toby moved to Nikki's seat. "Do you know how to contact Nicholas? Maybe it's time to talk to him."

"Yes, I know how to contact him. He left his number with Rachelle, but I'm not going to. There are too many negatives to letting him into our lives. It scares me, Tobe."

Her brother wrapped his arm around her shoulders. "I know it does, sweetheart, but Nikki needs to know her daddy and he needs to know her too. This isn't going to go away, you know. And the longer you leave it the harder it's going to be."

Prue let out a frustrated breath. "I know that, but it's far too complicated. Look, let's just enjoy the holidays together and then I'll give it some thought." *Maybe.*

Nineteen

When Prue arrived at work Monday morning one of the reception staff told her the talk show host had come down with a bad case of the flu, had no voice, and was home in bed. Prue was on the phone the minute she reached her desk. "Hello, Rachelle. How are you feeling?"

"Terrible," Rachelle croaked. "I feel like I'm dying."

"I'm sorry I disturbed you but I needed to know how you were. Do you need anything?"

"Thanks, but my sister's here." She coughed into the phone and sniffled. "I have to go. I'm aching all over and my throat is so sore. I'll try to email you later."

"Ok, take care of yourself. Be well soon."

Prue felt bad for her friend. She sounded dreadful. What could she do to cheer her up? She jumped online to send her some flowers with a Get Well Soon balloon attached. The bouquet she chose was so pretty and had all of the flowers Rachelle liked. She clicked the order button and a notification popped up telling her delivery would be the same afternoon. Prue smiled. *That should brighten Rachelle's day.*

Gabe came into her office. "Did you hear about Rachelle? Poor thing."

"Yes. I just sent her some get well flowers. I hope it helps her feel a bit better. She sounded terrible."

"Oh, you called her?"

Prue shrugged. "What are friends for?"

"True. Anyway, management is bringing in a well-known co-anchor for the week."

"Who?"

"If I tell you you'll have to keep it hush hush."

Prue frowned. "Why? Everyone will know when she arrives."

Gabe tsked and walked over to the doorway. "I know, lovely, but that's what I was told."

Prue moved around her desk and followed him. "Do you want me to swear?" She raised her hand.

Her colleague chuckled. "No need. I think you can be trusted." He whispered the name in her ear.

Prue's eyes widened. "Are you serious?"

"Came straight from the horse's mouth."

"She's someone I've looked up to my whole life. Did you know she was voted one of the fifty most beautiful people in the world by People magazine a few years ago?"

Gabe's eyebrows rose. "No, I didn't know that. Impressive."

"So we'll be working with her for a whole week's tapings? Ten shows?" Prue couldn't contain her excitement.

"That's the plan. We'll be doing three shows tomorrow, three Wednesday and two on Thursday and Friday. Lucky audience participants, huh?" Gabe strutted down the corridor then stopped and turned around. "Oh, by the way, she'll be here bright and early tomorrow morning."

Prue returned to her desk and sat down, her mind in a whirl. She would be working with Judy Finn for four days. What an incredible opportunity!

Later that afternoon, Prue received an email from Rachelle (typed by her sister) thanking her for the lovely flowers and asking for a favor. The talk show host had been invited to a Christmas charity dinner and auction for the Morgan Stanley Children's Hospital. It was a black tie affair with over five hundred guests: celebrities, authors, artists, musicians, high-ranking business CEOs and the general public. The event was being held at the Broad Street Ballroom, in the Financial District, Thursday evening at 7 p.m., and Rachelle couldn't go because she was far too ill and infectious. She asked Prue to stand in for her and told her she could borrow her Alyce Black Label evening gown for the occasion, if she was brave enough to come by and pick it up.

Even though Prue regretted that her best friend was lying ill in bed, she couldn't believe her good fortune. First, she would spend the next four days working beside one of TV's amazing and accomplished women, and two, she would get to attend a grand, black tie function, rubbing shoulders with the rich and famous. Her stomach did a nervous flip and she pinched herself to make sure she wasn't dreaming.

Prue was grateful for both opportunities and also that her brother was in town because he could babysit while she attended the event rather than her having to ask Yolanda. Her life had taken a sudden upturn and she was so happy. She shut down her computer, collected her belongings and headed for the stairs.

On the way home, Prue told her brother all about her

day and how Rachelle had asked her to attend the charity auction on her behalf because she was too ill. Toby seemed concerned about her and asked if she was alright. Prue told him Rachelle had a bad case of the flu and sounded dreadful, but if she knew her friend at all she would be back on her feet as soon as the antibiotics kicked in. She wondered if anyone at the studio had informed Rachelle of who was sitting in for her while she was away. That piece of news might just hasten her recovery.

Twenty

Prue put the finishing touches to her makeup while Yolanda fashioned her hair into a soft chignon. The style was perfect for the gorgeous dress Prue would be wearing. Rachelle's black and silver evening gown was sophisticated and stunning. The luxurious bodice had dazzling cap sleeves and featured sparkling crystal swirls over a delicate, skin tone transparent fabric. The silky, layered black chiffon skirt cascaded to the floor-length hemline, giving it an elegant ethereal appearance. It was divine, and, after trying it on the night before to make sure it was a perfect fit, Prue couldn't wait to wear it this evening.

Once her hair and makeup were done, Prue slipped into the delicate gown and slid her feet into a pair of strappy, five inch glittering silver heels. Yolanda had loaned her a set of chandelier earrings and necklace to match and Prue felt like a princess when she stepped up to the full-length mirror and saw her reflection. Tears of joy stung the backs of her eyes. She couldn't believe how lovely she looked.

After spraying the pulse points on her throat, between her breasts and on her wrists with Jádore perfume she opened the bedroom door, walked down the hallway into the living room and did a twirl.

Nikki drew in a surprised breath. "Oh, Mommy, you look like a beautiful princess."

Toby stood up and watched his sister twirl around. "You look stunning, sis. You're going to be beating men off with a stick."

Prue's cheeks flushed. "Thanks big brother. Nice to get a man's opinion."

Yolanda came up behind her. "Let me give your hair a light spray, just to hold it in place. There, now you're ready to go."

The doorbell rang and Yolanda opened the door.

"Good evening, I'm here to pick up Prue Granger," the limousine driver said. When he saw her his smile widened. "Are you ready Miss Granger?"

Prue felt like Cinderella going to the Prince's ball.

"Yes, I am. Thank you." She picked up her wrap and evening bag, kissed her daughter goodnight, and followed the driver down the stairs and out to the elegant black limousine waiting by the curb, courtesy of CBS. Her transformed pumpkin carriage. She sighed with happiness as the driver opened the door for her. *What a wonderful evening this is going to be.*

The limousine pulled into the curb directly opposite the triple brass doors and the driver stepped out of the car and opened the rear passenger door for Prue, offering his gloved hand to assist her out of the vehicle. Prue took his hand, lifted her skirt and stepped onto the red carpet adorning the sidewalk and leading into the columned building. Her heart did a little shudder as she gazed at her surroundings and the people entering the function. What an amazing night.

The driver gave her his card and said to call him at the number printed on it thirty minutes before pick up and he would arrive within that time to take her home. He tipped his hat and said, "Have a good evening, Miss," then returned to the limousine and eased into the traffic.

Prue swallowed the nervous lump in her throat, inhaled deeply, and entered the magnificent building.

The interior of the refurbished, austere, 1920s style bank building was incredible. Patterned Doric columns lined both sides of the expansive, subtly lit ballroom and around the walls a large mural, painted in 1929 by Griffith Baily Coale, depicted thirty-six generations of sailing ships. It took Prue's breath away. She had never been in such a magnificent room before.

Round banquet tables dotted the floor and were dressed with red covers, white place settings and red serviettes to match. The floral centerpieces were an assortment of red and white roses, yellow winter jasmine, baby's breath and leatherleaf ferns. They looked amazing.

A waiter carrying a tray of drinks stopped and handed Prue a champagne flute. She smiled, thanked him and took a sip of bubbly. She wandered the tables looking for her number and located it close to the stage. A front row seat. She was about to pull out her chair when a hand reached over and pulled it out for her. "Please, let me," the smooth voice said.

Prue glanced up and came face to face with gorgeous, in demand, actor Ty Kitson. "Thank you." She sat down and he joined her at her table.

"What's a beautiful woman like you doing here alone?" His smile was infectious.

"A last minute change of plans. My friend came down with the flu and couldn't make it." She sipped her champagne, her heart fluttering, and did her best to act sophisticated.

"Do you mind if I sit here for a while?" He swallowed the last mouthful of his drink.

"No, not at all." She held out her hand. "I'm Prue."

He took her hand. "Ty. Good to meet you."

She glanced around the tables. "Are you here with someone?"

"My date hasn't arrived yet. She was held up by a last minute change to a scene they're shooting."

"Oh. Well probably not a good idea to upset her when she does get here. I appreciate the offer, but I'm fine sitting by myself." She couldn't believe she was sending the handsome actor on his way. "Thanks though."

"If you're sure?" He gave her a curious frown.

Prue nodded. "I think it's best."

He smiled and stood up. "It's been a pleasure, although brief. Have a good evening."

"Thank you. You too. It's wonderful meeting you." She smiled.

The actor picked up his empty glass, gave her one last look and threaded his way through the tables to the bar.

Prue sighed. *Pity he wasn't on his own. Oh well.* She perused the evening's agenda and was in awe of the wonderful items celebrities, authors and artists had donated for such a worthy cause. Author J. P. Peterson had offered a signed copy of book one from each of his mystery series, singer *Crystal* provided a dazzling, red jeweled costume she'd worn on one of her world tours, actor Jay Dee donated a self-portrait, and rock band Minute by Minute provided a signed guitar. The list of incredible treasures went on and on.

Two middle-aged ladies, dressed to the nines, joined her table and introduced themselves. Prue did the same and they struck up a conversation. The room filled to capacity in no time and the noise level elevated. Guests were having a wonderful time and drinks flowed freely.

The lights flickered and everyone knew it was time to take their seats, the evening was about to begin. Prue felt butterflies in the pit of her stomach and took another sip of champagne. She had been given the option to bid if the item was noteworthy and would fit in the display cabinets adorning the foyer at the broadcast center.

Once the guests were seated, the emcee appeared on stage. "Good evening, everyone. My name is Gerry Buchanan. I'm only one of the many who organized this function. Later on, a list of all the volunteers who have given up their valuable time and have been nothing short of amazing will appear on the screen behind me. Thank you for being here tonight for such a worthy cause, The Morgan Stanley Children's Hospital. All of the proceeds from tonight's dinner and auction will assist with extensive research into life-threatening childhood diseases and to also bring some Christmas cheer to the seriously ill boys and girls who have to remain in the hospital while undergoing treatment during the holidays.

"I want to thank everyone who contributed. Without you this auction wouldn't have been possible. Your generosity is outstanding. We have some wonderful items on display over to your left, I hope you've taken the time to have a look and have chosen what you'll be bidding for tonight.

"Now for some general housekeeping. In the event of an emergency you will be directed to the nearest exit, which is highlighted by a red exit sign. Ladies and men's restrooms are on the right and appropriately signed. If you have any questions please come and see me or the door staff at the main entrance.

"Alright, without further ado, let's get this show on the road with Glenn Miller tribute band Serenade."

$\mathcal{T}$wenty one

After dinner guests left their tables and headed to the bar or the restrooms, whichever seemed more urgent. Prue remained in her seat at the empty table and when a waiter came by with flutes of champagne she asked for another glass and handed him her empty one.

During an earlier portion of the evening, the emcee had asked everyone to participate in an icebreaker by playing musical tables. Everyone would have until the music stopped to reach a table they wanted to sit at and three minutes to have a conversation with other guests before moving on to another table. Prue heard people saying "Sorry," "Excuse me," and "Hi, how are you? Let's catch up later," as they shuffled past other guests in the crowd. She managed to speak to a few celebs and artists on her way around and had even been given the phone number of one actress who had a daughter the same age as Nikki and asked her to catch up for coffee.

Prue was breathless as she gazed around the expansive ballroom in awe of how many celebrities had made an appearance at the event. What a wonderful turn out. Her cell phone buzzed inside her evening purse and she pulled it out to see who was calling. "Hello, Rachelle. Feeling any better?"

"I'm getting there, hon," she rasped, her throat still sore. "How's the evening going? Having fun?"

"It's amazing! I'm having a fantastic time. I'm so sorry you couldn't be here."

"Oh, don't worry about that. I'm glad you're enjoying yourself. Been swept off your feet by any handsome celebs yet?" She coughed and sniffled.

"Maybe not swept off my feet, but I did talk to Ty Kitson before the evening got started. He seems like a sweet guy. Unpretentious."

"Lucky you! He's hot too."

"Even more so in person." Prue giggled.

"I'd better go. I just wanted to make sure you were having a good time." She coughed. "My throat is so much sorer from talking. Have fun. See you when I'm not contagious."

"Take good care of yourself. I miss you." Prue tapped the screen and returned the phone to her evening bag. She glanced across the room at the display of donated items and wandered over to take a closer look. Would ten thousand dollars cover anything up for grabs? She didn't think so. And she wasn't sure she was comfortable spending someone else's money.

She began at the far left end of the long table and inched her way past each item, stopping to read the description from time to time. There were some valuable pieces that she thought would raise more than a few thousand dollars, and that was what the event was all about. Prue kept edging along until she was at the center. Some of the bigger items were displayed there: Jay Dee's painting, three signed guitars (from other bands and artists) and a number of movie props she recognized. How exciting.

Prue continued moving past the items and stopped when she came to an assortment of signed copies of famous author books. Her eyes ran over the selection and her breath caught in her throat when she noticed several Nicholas Colton novels among the group. She swung around and gazed up and down the huge room. *Is he here? He'd have to be, wouldn't he?* Prue's heart shuddered and her face flushed. There were over five hundred guests at the event and she hadn't seen him during the icebreaker. It didn't seem likely he would spot her amongst all those people, nonetheless she was anxious. Should she call for the limousine and leave?

Before she had time to make up her mind she heard his voice behind her.

"Hello." He couldn't believe she was standing in front of him.

Prue closed her eyes, inhaled deeply, then opened her eyes, put on her best smile and turned around. "Hello."

Nicholas scanned the ballroom searching for the tall man she had been with at the Halloween party.

His eyes returned to her. "Are… are you here with anyone?"

Prue wasn't sure how to answer. Would she lie and say she was or tell him the truth? She knew she couldn't lie. "No, I'm on my own. You?"

"I'm here alone too. How are you?"

"I'm well. How are you?" She hated small talk and wondered how she could remove herself from the uncomfortable situation without appearing rude.

"Busy. I'm an author and I'm currently working on my next novel."

"Oh. That's…"

"Can I ask your name?" The words came out before he could stop them and a look of uncertainty crossed his face. He gave her a charming smile to mask his emotions.

"We did agree to anonymity, remember?" Prue felt a nervous lump thickening in her throat, she couldn't breathe. *Why does this keep happening?* Maybe Rachelle was right. Serendipity was toying with her.

"That was so long ago." He held out his hand. "Hi, I'm Nicholas. It's wonderful to see you again."

She gazed at his hand but didn't take it. Tears stung her eyes and she blinked them back. "I think it's best to leave things as they are. Don't you?"

Nicholas stepped forward. "But why?" He didn't want to lose her again.

Prue stepped back. "Because we're two different people now."

"Are we? I don't see that."

"I'm sorry." She turned on her stilettoed heel and threaded her way through the tables as fast as she could, heading for the main entrance, tears sliding down her face.

"Please wait." Nicholas followed her out to the street.

Prue snatched her cell phone and the driver's card out of her purse and fumbled to press the number into the keypad. "H – Hello?" She stopped. Nicholas was only a few feet away. She was trapped with no way to escape. She hung up.

He came up behind her. "Can we please talk? That's all I'm asking."

Prue shivered and pulled her sheer wrap around her shoulders. The chilly night air drifted through the delicate fabric of her gown connecting with her jangled nerves. "There's nothing to say. We needed each other for one night. Let's not make more of it than it actually was." She hated herself for saying such a thing, knowing in her heart she had fallen in love with him all those years ago.

Nicholas frowned at her. "Is that how you really feel?" He had hoped she regretted not telling him her name and how she might have felt. Perhaps she hadn't felt anything at all. Perhaps he was the only one who had fallen in love that night.

Prue nodded. "How am I supposed to feel? We both agreed to one night without emotional strings. And you're right it was such a long time ago." Her heart pounded against her breastbone and she couldn't take a breath. She knew she was lying to him and to herself, but as much as her heart told her to she couldn't allow him into her life. She had to protect her daughter.

The look of desperation on Nicholas' face almost unraveled her resolve but she couldn't allow it to, she had to stay strong. She knew everything would change if she didn't.

"I thought…" He gave a heavy sigh. "I had hoped you'd feel differently."

Prue frowned. "Why?"

His eyes met hers. "Because I fell in love with you that night and I hoped you'd fallen in love with me too. We had a deeper connection than just sex. I felt it. Didn't you?"

That had been what he'd wanted to say when he looked across the hotel room at her. Prue had the overwhelming desire to run into his arms and tell him how she truly felt, but she wouldn't. Too much was at stake.

The driver must have recognized Prue's phone number because the limousine pulled into the curb in front of her and the driver opened the back passenger door.

"Take care of yourself, Nicholas. Goodbye." Prue climbed into the elegant sedan.

Nicholas stood on the red carpeted sidewalk and watched her leave his life once again, still knowing nothing about her except that she had captured his heart and there was nothing he could do about it.

More tears spilled down Prue's face and she sniffed back the urge to sob. Was she crazy for letting the man she loved, and who loved her, walk out of her life? Yes, but there was no other way. Nothing she could do would change that. She had lost so much once before and wasn't about to let that happen again. She fumbled in her purse for a tissue and dabbed her cheeks. The driver frowned into the rearview mirror for a moment then asked, "Everything alright, Miss Granger?"

The lump in her throat prevented her from answering and she gave a nod.

He wasn't convinced. "Are you sure? Is there something I can do?"

Prue shook her head.

"If you need anything just let me know. Ok?"

She nodded and blew her nose. Tears continued to spill.

Once again Prue felt like Cinderella, only this time she was running away from her handsome prince without leaving a glass slipper for him to follow.

Twenty two

Nicholas sat on his front porch gazing out at the impending storm clouds rolling in. The day had become as gray as his mood and he gave a heavy sigh. The scene he'd imagined in his head where he'd find the woman he was in love with and she would run into his arms and tell him she loved him too had taken a dramatic plot twist. How could he rewrite the story so it worked in his favor? He was still in the dark as to who she was, even though he had the sketch, and had no idea how to find her. It was strange how they had bumped into each other twice in such a small space of time, after all these years. Did he believe in serendipity? Were the fates at work here? Maybe.

Benji was in the house and Rocky was lying by his feet. He thought how lucky dogs were because they didn't fall in love and run the risk of having their hearts broken. He had been devastated when his wife passed away, he never thought his heart would mend, then he met her. Their night together had opened his eyes and his heart and when he walked out of that hotel room he knew he'd made the biggest mistake of his life. But he was a man of honor. They had agreed to a night with no strings and he had kept to that agreement.

Nicholas knew he should have turned around, walked back through that door, took her in his arms and told her he loved her. He should have asked to see her again. Have dinner. Get to know one another. But he hadn't. What a fool he'd been.

His cell phone jingled beside him and he checked the caller ID. It was Peter.

"Hey, buddy, what can I do for you?" He noticed lightning flashing in the distance. The storm would hit in the next hour or so.

"Can I stop by? I've got something I want to tell you in person."

"Sure." Nicholas straightened in his chair. "Sounds serious."

"Put the coffee on. I'll see you in ten." He rang off.

Nicholas frowned at his phone then pulled himself

out of the comfortable, padded wicker armchair and headed into the house to the kitchen. Rocky followed him.

Peter arrived twelve minutes later and let himself in. "Hey, Nick, I'm here," he called.

"In the kitchen."

The PI wandered through the living room and into the hub of the house. Nicholas was sitting at the breakfast table with two mugs of coffee and a plate of chocolate chip cookies he'd baked himself. He stood up and shook his friend's hand. "What's going on?" He returned to his seat.

Peter sat down opposite him and picked up a cookie. "You bake these?"

"Yeah."

"I love your cookies." He took a bite.

"Want to tell me why you're here?" Nicholas gave him an impatient frown.

"I got a guy I know at the DMV to run the sketch Colin did of your mystery woman."

Nicholas' heartrate ticked up a notch. "And?"

He slid the printout across the table. "He found her Pittsburgh driver's license."

Nicholas opened the piece of paper and smiled. There she was. His eyes wandered her beautiful face before skimming over the information. Prue Lorraine Granger. At last he had a name. He glanced up at his friend. "I can't believe I finally know who she is. How can I ever repay you?"

Peter picked up another cookie from off the plate and held it up. "You could make me a batch of these some time, they're delicious."

"Absolutely. I'll make you two dozen. How's that?"

"Freakin' awesome." Peter took a large bite of his cookie.

"What should I do now?"

"If she doesn't want to talk to you, you need to tread carefully. You don't want to be labelled a stalker, not with your respectable New York Times author reputation." He swallowed a mouthful of black coffee to wash down the cookie. "It's odd that she doesn't have another state's driver's license. You think she's in New York, right?"

Nicholas nodded. "Yeah, I've seen her there a couple of times now. Maybe she doesn't drive anymore."

Peter gave him a doubtful look. "If she drove in Pittsburgh you'd think she'd drive in New York."

"Driving in Pittsburgh is different to New York. Maybe she feels overwhelmed by big city traffic."

"Maybe."

"Is there any way to find out where she works?"

Peter shook his head. "Not unless you know someone at the IRS who'd be willing to give you the information."

Nicholas sighed. "Unfortunately, no." He always seemed to hit a dead end where Prue—he could say her name—was concerned. At least he had something substantial to go on now. It was a starting point.

"Just remember what I said. If you find her and she files a complaint against you, you could be looking at criminal charges. And that's something you don't want."

"I'll remember. I just need to get her to talk to me."

"She didn't want to at the dinner you attended. What makes you think she'll want to now?"

"Call it intuition. What she was telling me at the dinner didn't match the emotion in her eyes or her body language. Something was off."

"Or you want to believe something was off." He took another mouthful of his coffee.

"Ok, maybe. I have to know for sure." Nicholas gazed at her photo again. "I'm in love with her, Pete, and I can't change how I feel."

His friend gave him a pained look. "Love can suck sometimes. I hope it works out the way you want it to."

Nicholas gave him a thin smile. "Me too, buddy. Me too."

Twenty three

December twenty third came around in the blink of an eye and Prue still had to organize packing for their trip. Toby would arrive some time in the early afternoon and she wanted to have the apartment looking and smelling Christmassy by then. She and Nikki had already hung the decorations around the apartment while listening to a selection of carols on her MacBook, including Nikki's favorites, Frosty the Snowman and Rudolf the Red nosed Reindeer. The tree had arrived the week before, but they hadn't dressed the wonderfully, scented green spruce yet.

Prue sat the box of ornaments on the coffee table and called Nikki. Her daughter raced out of her bedroom and joined her in the living room. "Can I put the Christmas angel on top, Mommy?"

"Yes you can, honey." Prue fossicked through the assortment of delicate pieces and handed a crystal snowflake to Nikki. She had already threaded the lights through the branches so it was just a matter of decorating now. "Where would you like this one to go?"

Nikki took the sparkling, star-shaped decoration and stood for a moment contemplating where the first piece should be placed. She reached out and hung it on a branch in the center of the tree, then stepped back to see how it looked. "Is that ok, Mommy?"

"It's perfect."

The pair continued to work on the tree until the last decoration had been hung on a bough. Prue handed the beautiful golden angel, blowing a trumpet to herald the birth of Christ, to her daughter then lifted her up so she could place it on top. Once the angel was in position they both stepped back to examine their handy work.

Nikki clapped and bobbed up and down like a Jack-in-the-Box. "Don't forget the lights, Mommy."

Prue stepped around the tree to the power outlet and flicked the switch. The twinkling white lights sent a shimmer through the delicate crystal ornaments making them sparkle in a kaleidoscope of color that radiated onto the corner wall behind the tree. It looked wonderful.

"Yay!" Nikki said. "It's beautiful, Mommy."

Prue picked up her little girl and they stood admiring the glittering tree. "Yes, it is, sweetie."

The light dusting of snow lying on the windowsills gave the scene a pretty winter feel. It was freezing outside. Pittsburgh was a slightly warmer city and Prue couldn't wait to be home with her mom, dad and other relatives.

Her cell phone went off: Jingle bells, jingle bells, jingle all the way. "Hello."

"Hi, it's me," Toby said. "I should arrive at your place around three. Got eggnog? If not, I'll pick some up at a store on the way."

"Already made mom's recipe."

"Yum, can't wait. Ok, well, better keep moving. See you in a couple hours."

"Take care on the road, Tobe."

"Yep, will do." He rang off.

"Is Uncle Toby going to be here soon?"

"He should get here around three, so let's go bake those Christmas cookies."

The aroma of cinnamon sugar cookies gave the apartment a warming Christmas feel. When Toby arrived they would sit down to afternoon tea of cookies, turkey and cranberry sandwiches and eggnog. Prue had concocted a kid-friendly version of the drink for her daughter so she wouldn't feel left out of the holiday celebrations.

Nicholas' face popped into her head as she set the table and she wondered what his plans were for the holidays. Did he have family to go home to? Would he spend them alone? Her heart felt heavy for a moment and she hoped he had someone to spend Christmas with.

A knock on the door brought Nikki flying out of her room. "Uncle Toby's here!" She skidded down the hallway in her socks and almost collided with her mom.

Prue opened the front door and her daughter launched herself at her uncle. "Yay, you're here. We're having afternoon tea, Uncle Toby." She kissed his cheek, wrapped her arms around his neck and gave him a big squeeze.

"We are? That sounds great." He popped his niece onto the floor, kissed his sister's cheek and inhaled a deep breath through his nostrils. "What's the wonderful smell?"

"Nikki and I made your favorite. Iced cinnamon sugar cookies."

"Well what are we waiting for? Let's go eat." Toby kicked the overnight bag out of the way, closed the door, followed his two favorite girls into the living/dining room and sat down at the decorated table.

Prue and Nikki took their seats and Prue poured eggnog and the special eggnog for Nikki into glasses and handed them around. She raised hers. "To the love of family and to spending Christmas together."

"To the love of family and to spending Christmas together," Toby and Nikki chorused, clinking their glasses.

Prue's heart felt light and she was looking forward to the drive home with her daughter and her big brother. It was going to be a wonderful holiday.

Twenty four

Nicholas' parents had retired to Kennedy Township, Pennsylvania and he was on his way to spend the holidays with them. Three years ago they had purchased a quaint, timber two-story home with attic on an acre block and loved living in the peaceful rural community. His sister, Connie and her family lived in Santa Barbara and would also be making the journey. It had been a couple of years since Nicholas had been home for Christmas, work commitments had kept him busy, and he was looking forward to spending time with his family this year.

The flight from Monterey to Pittsburgh would take about six and a half hours, so Nicholas kept himself busy working on the outline for his next novel. He realized he did a great deal of plotting and writing on airplanes because of the time it took flying from one side of the country to the other. His parents were picking him up from the airport at around 4.30 p.m. in time for a late afternoon tea. His mom had made his favorite festive treats and he felt like a schoolboy again.

He missed her. He missed them all. It would be great being with them again, especially his sister, brother-in-law, niece and nephew, whom he hadn't seen for the past three years because they were unable to make Christmas the last time he'd been home as Connie had gone into early labor with Addison. It would be lovely meeting his niece in person for the first time. He loved kids. He and Pam had planned to have a house full when they were first married, but that wasn't to be. After she had been diagnosed with a brain tumor and underwent treatments of chemotherapy there was no way she could carry a child. Her body couldn't have handled it. Tears stung the backs of his eyes and he dislodged the painful memory from his mind. It was Christmas, the season to be jolly.

Nicholas intended to maintain the holiday spirit while visiting his parents. No brooding over the past or Prue—although both were a constant ache in his heart—as his mom always picked up on his moods and would be sure to quiz him about what was wrong. Christmas was a time for family and he was going to adhere to keeping his love life woes private. He had made a promise to himself that once the holidays were over he'd fly to New York to find the woman he loved and when he did he wouldn't take no for an answer. She had to talk to him.

☙ ♥ ❧

When Toby pulled his dual cab Dodge pickup into their parents' driveway and turned off the engine the front door flew open and Lorraine and Martin Granger came rushing out, arms wide. Nikki flung the back door of the truck open and jumped from the vehicle into the waiting arms of her grandma and grandpa. "Grandma, Poppie," the little girl squealed. "I missed you so much."

"We missed you too, honey," Her grandma said, hugging her tight. She handed her granddaughter to her husband and walked over to her daughter. "Merry Christmas. How are you, darling?" She wrapped her arms around Prue and held her for a long moment. "It's so good to have you home."

"Merry Christmas, Mom. It's wonderful to be home." She glanced over at her dad. "Merry Christmas, Daddy"

He smiled. "Merry Christmas, Sweet Pea."

"Let's go inside. We've got a fire going and it's nice and warm," her mom said.

"You all go. I'll bring in the bags." Toby pulled the luggage from the tray of his truck and carried it up onto the porch, then returned for the box of Christmas presents and baking.

The house smelled of Pine cones and cinnamon. A real holiday aroma. Prue hung hers and Nikki's coats on the rack by the front door and helped her brother bring in the bags.

Once the front door closed and she stood in the decorated entry hall of her parents' home she sighed with happiness.

"Come into the kitchen you two. We've got Christmas goodies to devour," their mother called.

When Prue and Toby entered the kitchen, Nikki was already on a stool at the center island with a glass of milk in front of her, munching a reindeer cookie.

Prue walked over to her. "I used to love these when I was your age. Still do." She reached across and plucked a cookie from the plate sitting in the middle of the counter and took a bite. "Mm, heavenly."

"Coffee's ready. Help yourself," her father said.

Toby crossed the kitchen to the coffee maker, poured four mugs and brought them back to the center island. "Here you go. Enjoy."

They sat talking, laughing and eating for a good couple of hours before Prue climbed off her stool to go unpack the presents and place them under the huge, dazzling Christmas tree standing by the arched, multi-pained window in the living room. Afterward, she sat the baking she had done on the kitchen counter. Tomorrow the house would be filled with family and friends and holiday cheer. As far back as Prue could remember her mother always had a large, festive Christmas dinner with tons of food and plenty of people. But tonight it would be only them and she couldn't wait to sit around the fire with her family drinking her mother's special eggnog and relaxing. Coming home had been the stabilizing factor to her crazy year and she felt peaceful and happy.

A thin blanket of white freeze lay across the tarmac as Nicholas' flight landed at Pittsburgh International. Three snow ploughs were working to clear the runways, plumes of snow spraying behind them like frosty waterfalls. It looked pretty from his window, but he knew how cold it would be once he stepped off the plane.

While he waited for other passengers to disembark, Nicholas thought about the night he'd spent with Prue, and how strange it had been that his parents decided to move there. Well, not right in Pittsburgh itself, but they were only twenty minutes by car from the main city center. The word serendipity popped into his head and once again he wondered if the fates were somehow trying to bring him and Prue together. His heart soared when he thought about how wonderful it would be to hold her in his arms again.

After collecting his luggage, Nicholas headed for the pickup area outside the baggage claim. His parents should already be there.

He stepped out into the icy air and shivered as he scanned the cars driving in to pick up family and friends. His dad's four wheel drive wasn't there. He checked his watch and frowned. 4.28 p.m. Maybe they pulled into the short term parking garage. Retrieving his cell phone from the pocket of his insulated, charcoal gray Adidas jacket he hit speed dial.

"Hey, Dad, I'm outside the baggage claim. Where are you? I can make my way over to you, if you'd prefer."

"We're in the short term parking lot. Stay there, we'll pick you up."

"Ok. See you soon."

Several minutes later, Nicholas spotted his parents' silver Jeep traveling up the center lane and he grabbed his bags, ready to toss them in the trunk. He was looking forward to sitting in a nice warm car out of the chilly wind. When his father pulled up he climbed out of the car and gave Nicholas a man hug. "Great to see you, son."

"You too, Dad."

They dropped the luggage into the back of the car and climbed into the warm cabin, Nicholas behind his mom's seat. She turned around and squeezed his hand, her face beaming. "It's good to have you home, Nick."

"It's good to be home. I know it's been a while."

"We understand, honey. You have a busy life." Ashleigh held up his latest book. "Love this one."

Nicholas felt his face grow warm. He didn't think his mother read novels of his genre. He thought about the lovemaking scene and wondered what she thought when she read it, but wouldn't ask. "Glad you liked it."

"I'm still reading it. I only bought it yesterday, but it's a real page turner. I've been so engrossed your father says I'm neglecting him." She laughed.

His dad's eyes met his in the rearview mirror. "She's so taken with your book I never see her."

"Sorry about that." He smiled.

"Ah, no need to be sorry, son. Your books are fantastic. I should know, I've read 'em all. Well, except this new one. But I plan to after your mom finishes with it," Evan told him.

Nicholas was surprised that his parents were reading his books. But, then again, why should he be. Both were avid readers. They had raised him to love books and he believed that was the reason he became a writer.

"You know, you could've asked me to mail you a copy so you didn't have to pay for it."

His mom waved the comment off. "No way. Book sales are book sales. And I was happy to buy it. You'll have to sign it for me later."

"Sure." His mom asking him to sign her book felt weird but nice.

They chatted on the way home about everything from books, to Christmas, to Connie coming home, to what his parents had been doing on their property, to who Nicholas was dating. He told his parents he wasn't seeing anyone, which was the truth, and omitted to mention Prue. He wanted to keep the pact he had made with himself about not discussing his love life dramas over the holidays. Even so, Prue's face still hovered in the back of his thoughts and he wondered what her plans were for Christmas.

Twenty five

Prue could smell something burning and raced into the kitchen. She rushed over, grabbed a dish towel and pushed the saucepan off the stove top. The cranberry sauce had congealed to black goo and was stuck to the sides and bottom of the utensil. Where was her mom? "Mom? Mom, where are you?" Prue checked the laundry then went to the back door. Her dad was outside collecting firewood but her mother wasn't with him. "Dad, where's mom?" she called.

Her father shook his head and went back to loading the small cart with logs.

Prue wandered through the house. She checked the living room. No one. She walked through to the dining room. Still no one. She headed back to the study, opened the door and peered inside. Her mom was sitting behind the desk on the telephone discussing plans for their big Christmas dinner the following day.

"There you are. I…"

Her mother raised a finger for Prue to stop talking. "Ok. I'll look forward to it. See you then." She hung up the receiver. "Sorry about that, honey. Just organizing a few things with people who are coming for dinner tomorrow. Now, what's up?"

Prue sighed. "I hate to tell you this but your cranberry sauce burned."

"Oh no." Lorraine sprang out of the desk chair and raced out of the room. Prue followed. "I thought I had it on simmer." She rushed across the kitchen to the saucepan. "Oh dear, look at that. I don't have enough cranberries to make another batch." She turned to Prue. "What am I going to do?"

Toby and Nikki came into the kitchen. "What's that God awful smell?" Toby said, wrinkling his nose.

Prue shook her head and frowned at him. "Mom's cranberry sauce burned."

Nikki ran over to Lorraine and wrapped her arms around her hips. "Sorry your sauce burned, Grandma."

"Can't you make some more?" Toby's logical question was scowled at by both women.

"I could if I had enough cranberries and sugar, but I don't," Lorraine told him, folding her arms.

"Well, hell, that's easy fixed. I'll just take a drive into town and pick up some more," her son said.

Lorraine glanced at the kitchen clock. It was 4.30 p.m. "It's Christmas Eve. Stores won't be open late tonight."

"I'll jump on the Expressway and be there in no time. How much do you need?"

"Uh, well, I'll need four 12 ounce bags of frozen cranberries and two pounds of sugar." She crossed the kitchen. "Just wait one minute and I'll give you the money."

"It's fine, Mom, I can get it." He headed out of the kitchen.

Prue took after him. "Can I come for the ride?"

Toby shrugged into his suede jacket. "Sure. I'd enjoy the company."

Prue grabbed her coat, scarf and knit cap and followed her brother out to his truck.

❦

Most of the stores were already closed as Toby and Prue drove through Pittsburgh's city center. Finding somewhere open looked grim as they continued along the main street. Prue checked the opening hours for the local Shop 'n Save on Center Avenue, hoping it was still open. "Tobe, the Shop 'n Save closes at five. It's seven minutes to. Take the next left."

At five minutes to five Toby's Dodge screeched into the parking space near the front entrance and he and Prue raced inside. Store security was already at the door and the pair thought they were too late.

"Is it ok to go on in?" Toby asked.

"It's Christmas Eve. We're about to close. Just waiting on the last few shoppers."

"We'll be quick. Promise." Prue gave him her sweetest smile.

The guy sighed and waved them through. "Go on."

"Thank you. Merry Christmas," Prue said.

Toby rushed through the supermarket to the freezer section for the cranberries while Prue headed for the baking aisle to grab the sugar. They met at the checkout.

"That was close. If we'd been a couple minutes later that guy wouldn't have let us in." Prue was out of breath.

"You're not kidding." Toby placed the items down and the girl ran them through the scanner.

On the way out the door Prue heard someone call her

name. She thought it must be an old friend or a previous acquaintance until she turned around.

She glanced up at her brother. "Oh no."

Nicholas hurried up to them.

Toby took the shopping bag from her hand. "I'll give you a minute, sweetheart." He walked over to the truck and climbed in. The author watched him.

Prue frowned at Nicholas. "How do you know my name? And what are you doing here?"

His eyes returned to her and he looked sheepish. "My best friend is a private investigator. He found your driver's license on the DMV website. My parents live in Kennedy. I'm here to spend Christmas with them."

Prue didn't know what to say. She stood frowning at the author, wondering if he was telling the truth.

"Look, I'm not stalking you, if that's what you're thinking. We just happen to be in the same place at the same time, once again. I'd like to talk to you. Can we make some time to meet after the holidays?"

Prue didn't want to commit to meeting him. She needed her life to remain as it was. "I... don't know."

He reached for her hand. "Please, Prue."

She eased her gloved hand out of his. "I don't think it's a good idea."

"Why? What can happen from us talking?"

Prue sighed. "Ok."

Nicholas took out his wallet and handed her a business card. "My cell number's on there. Will you call me after the holidays?"

Prue glanced at the card. "I'm not sure when exactly, but I'll call."

He frowned. "You're not putting me off, are you?"

She shook her head. "No, of course not. I will call you. I just can't give you an exact date."

"Could we do it while we're both here?"

"I can't make any promises. I'm here with my family. So are you. Let's…"

"Play it by ear?" He looked skeptical.

Prue huffed. "Alright. Saturday. Does that suit you?"

The tension drained from Nicholas' face. "Yes, it does. Where and when?"

"Twenty First St Coffee and Tea on Fifth at ten." Her pulse quickened. She was actually going to sit down with this man and have a full-length conversation. It elated her and scared her at the same time.

The smile of joy on his face was evident. Prue had caused that. She wondered if he'd be smiling once she told him he had a five year old daughter. Would she tell him?

On the drive home Prue told Toby about the conversation she'd had with the author and asked him if he thought she had done the right thing. In her heart she felt as though she had but in her head she knew nothing good could come from it. Once Nicholas knew about Nikki things would change forever.

"You know you're doing the right thing, sis."

Prue gave a heavy sigh. "Am I? Everything will change if I tell him about Nikki. It could get ugly, you know. What if he wants joint custody? What if he takes me to court?"

Toby rested his hand on hers. "You're jumping to conclusions. Give the man a chance."

Prue scowled. "To ruin our lives, you mean?"

"Do you believe that?"

"I don't know. I have no idea what kind of man he is. Rachelle said he's a nice man, but nice men can do nasty things too."

"Why not wait until you have the conversation with him and see how you feel then. You don't have to tell him anything right away. Just keep it relaxed."

"You're right." The frown disappeared from her face. "It'll be a friendly chat over coffee. Nothing more."

*T*wenty six

Christmas morning, Nikki was up before the sun rose. She flung the door open to her mom's room and shouted with excitement, "It's Christmas! Come see what Santa brought us." Then raced along the hall to her grandparents' room and the guest room where Toby was sleeping. Everyone, now jolted from sleep, climbed out of bed, wrapped themselves in their warm robes and followed the little girl downstairs to the living room.

Nikki bobbed up and down clapping her hands. "Look at all the lovely presents. We must've all been good this year."

Lorraine stepped up beside her. "Why don't we sit down and I'll pass the presents around. How does that sound?"

"Ok, Grandma."

Everyone made themselves comfortable on the sofa and in the armchairs and Lorraine began handing out presents. "Now who is this one for? Let me see." She pulled her glasses from the pocket of her robe and placed them on her nose. "Oh, it's for Nikki." She passed the large gift to her granddaughter. "Merry Christmas, sweetie."

Nikki snatched the pretty package from her grandma's hands, her eyes wide. "Merry Christmas, Grandma." She pulled the huge glittering bow off the gift and ripped at the colorful wrapping.

Lorraine continued to hand out presents.

"Yay! It's just want I wanted," Nikki shouted with glee when she saw the Discovery Kids Laptop Computer. "Thank you, Mommy." Her face beamed. "I love it."

"You're welcome, honey." Prue opened her gift from Nikki. It was a hand-painted picture frame that her daughter had made at preschool with a picture of the two of them inside it. A tear trickled down Prue's cheek and she brushed it away before anyone noticed. "I love this, sweetie. It's beautiful."

Nikki's smile widened and she ran over to her mom and hugged her tight. "I knew you would, Mommy. It's just us."

Prue glanced at her brother sitting in an armchair across from her and mouthed 'Am I doing the right thing?'

He nodded and mouthed back, 'Later.'

Once all the presents had been unwrapped it was time for breakfast.

"We'd better get the place warmed up, it's cold in here," Martin said, rubbing his hands together. He pulled himself out of his armchair and set about making a fire.

Lorraine headed for the stairs. "Be back in a couple minutes to start breakfast. How does waffles with scrambled eggs, bacon and maple syrup sound?"

Everyone couldn't wait.

Prue followed her mother upstairs, Nikki in tow. "We'll help once we're dressed."

Christmas day had started out wonderfully and Prue knew it would only get better.

❦

Nicholas was out on the front porch sipping a mug of steaming black coffee when his sister appeared beside him. "Morning, little brother."

"Morning." He turned around to face her. "Addison is such a little sweetheart. Not to say Braydon isn't too, but something about my niece just melts my heart."

Connie smiled. "She is an angel. You know, she's never been any bother. She has always been a contented little girl from day one."

Nicholas' expression turned somber. "I had hoped for a daughter one day. A little princess."

Connie rested a hand on her brother's arm. "I know. It'll happen. You'll see."

"I hope so. I'd love to be a dad."

"You will be. You just need to find the right woman. How's that going, by the way?"

Nicholas sighed. "I haven't dated at all since…"

"Well you should. You're a good-looking guy there has to be someone out there for you."

A fleeting thought crossed his mind to tell her about Prue, but he decided against it.

"I'm so busy with deadlines and book signings and interviews I don't really have the time to date."

"Make time. It's the only way you're going to meet someone, fall in love and start a family. You're not getting any younger."

"Yeah, I know. But I'll always be younger than you." Nicholas grinned and poked his sister in the ribs.

Connie chuckled. "That's true, *little* brother." She frowned. "You looked like you were going to say something before but changed your mind. Have you already met someone?"

Nicholas felt his face grow warm. Connie was like his mother. She could tell when he had something on his mind. "No. Well… maybe."

Connie linked an arm through his. "Do tell."

"I made a promise to myself that I wasn't going to discuss my love life. Maybe we should stick to that."

"Tell your big sister," she coaxed.

He frowned. "This has to be between us, ok? I don't want anyone else in the family to know about it."

Connie crossed her heart. "You have my word."

Nicholas knew her word was her bond. She had kept many a secret for him when they were growing up.

He glanced at the front door. "Where is everybody?"

"Mom and dad are in the kitchen gearing up for a hearty breakfast and Lloyd is upstairs with the kids."

They sat in the swing seat along the porch.

Nicholas looked out at the impending dawn. The sun's weak winter rays peered over the tops of the trees. "About five years ago I met a woman at Hemingway's Café. I sat down beside her at the bar during happy hour and offered to buy her a drink. I don't think either of us had done anything like it before." He sighed.

"After an hour of idle conversation we ended up in a hotel room. Not my finest moment, I know, but I needed her, needed to feel desired again, and she seemed to need that too. We'd made an agreement to one night with no names and no strings. Now that I look back on it, it was the stupidest thing I'd ever done."

Connie gave him a sympathetic look and squeezed his hand.

"We did the deed and never saw each other again until a couple of months ago in LA. Since then I've seen her twice. I talked to her briefly last night and she agreed to meet me Saturday to talk. The only problem is I think she's with someone. I've seen him with her twice now and I thought she was with him in LA too."

"So what are you going to do?"

"Good question." He covered her hand with his. "I know I'm in love with her, Con. Stupid, huh?"

Connie shook her head. "No, it's not stupid. You had a very intimate connection."

"Yeah, we did. More than you could know. But maybe I was the only one who fell in love that night. Although, when I talked to her at the benefit in New York there was something in her eyes that didn't agree with what she said."

"What did she say?"

Nicholas frowned. "It was better to leave things the way they were."

"Oh. But she's going to meet up with you on Saturday, right?"

"Yes. At least I hope so. I hope she doesn't stand me up and leave me sitting at that café all morning."

❧ ♥ ☙

Christmas day had been perfect with no thoughts of Nicholas Colton entering Prue's mind. Spending time with her loved ones and family friends had been the best medicine. She felt at peace as she stood on her parents' front porch gazing up at the twinkling stars peeking through the clouds. Her stomach was full and her mind was at rest.

Toby opened the front door, grabbed his jacket and stepped outside. "Nice night, huh?"

"Yep. Beautiful." She smiled.

"Dinner was great."

"Dinner was super delicious. And some. Mom's an amazing cook."

"Yeah, she is." He waited a beat. "How are you feeling about Saturday?"

The question pulled a tight knot in the pit of Prue's stomach and the calmness she had felt was replaced with instant tension. "I'm thinking of canceling."

Toby crossed the porch and stepped up beside her. "Why? You don't have to admit anything. Hear the man out, sweetheart. It'll be good for the both of you."

"What if he already knows about Nikki? What if his PI friend found out about her? Maybe he wants to ambush me into admitting the truth and then tell me he's going to claim custody rights." Her heartbeat ticked up a notch.

"Was he upset or angry when he spoke to you?"

Prue gave her brother a sideward glance. "Well, no. He seemed genuinely happy to see me and said he only wanted to talk."

Toby wrapped his arm around Prue's shoulders and pulled her to him. "So talk."

Twenty seven

Saturday morning came around way too fast and when Prue opened her eyes and glanced at the bedside clock she was shocked to see that it was already eight o'clock. Her mom must have looked after Nikki and allowed her some sleep in time. She threw back the covers and rushed into the bathroom for a quick shower. She felt less frazzled when she walked back into her room wrapped in her snug winter robe, towel drying her hair.

Prue wondered what she should wear. Should she apply makeup? Should she dress in something other than her jeans and sweater, jacket and knit cap? What would they talk about? Would he ask her what her life has been like since that night? Would he want to know if she was in a relationship? The more she thought about it the harder it seemed and she had the overwhelming inclination to call and cancel. Toby's words once again rang in her ears, 'Hear the man out. It'll be good for the both of you.'

Would it?

A knock on the door made Prue jump and it took a second for her to gather her composure. She inhaled a deep breath and let it out. "Come in," she called.

The door opened and her mother came into the room with a mug of coffee. "Thought you could use a heart starter. Breakfast is waiting for you downstairs when you're ready," she said, setting the mug on the bedside table. "I took Nikki downstairs and gave her breakfast about two hours ago, so she's all sorted. She's in the living room with her uncle watching Dora the Explorer."

"Thanks, Mom, I really appreciate it. I don't get a chance to sleep in at home. Nikki's up at the crack of dawn every day. It was nice. But I do have to go into town for a bit. I'm having coffee with an old friend."

"Oh, that'll be nice. So I won't expect you back for lunch then?"

"Not sure. I might be back. Can I text you?"

Her mother raised an eyebrow. "You can call me."

Prue smiled. "Yeah, ok. I'll call and let you know."

Lorraine gave Prue a light hug and headed for the door. "Lunch is at one."

Prue took a sip of her coffee and went back to deciding what to wear. It wasn't a date so she didn't have to dress up, but she felt she should look her best. After ten minutes of standing at her closet undecided she went downstairs to eat breakfast. A full stomach might be the fuel she needed to make a choice and stick with it.

When Prue returned to her room, she chose a mid-length black skirt, an apricot cashmere sweater, black knee high boots and a gray wool jacket to coordinate the look. She dried and styled her hair with soft loose curls and applied a light coat of makeup. She'd wear her knit cap because it was freezing outside and take it off once she got to the café.

Toby offered to drive her, but Prue said she thought it best that she go alone. She borrowed her mother's bright blue Ford Focus and headed off at a quarter after nine. She wanted to be the first to arrive at the coffee shop.

Her heart raced as she sped along the Expressway and she couldn't take a breath. Was she doing the right thing? Would this meeting cause drama in their lives that none of them needed? She pulled into the breakdown lane, her doubts getting the better of her. The what ifs outweighed the what could bes. Prue plucked her cell phone from her purse and fossicked through her bag for the card Nicholas had given her. She keyed in his number and her thumb hovered over the button. Should she cancel? Did she really want to? Her heart played tug of war with her emotions. She was in love with the man so why was she making it so difficult for herself?

Prue dropped the phone back into her purse, indicated, and pulled out onto the highway once it was safe to do so. She gave a heavy sigh as she continued toward Downtown Pittsburgh and hoped she'd made the right decision.

Nicholas checked his watch. 9:40. His nerves were on edge as he sat inside the coffee shop waiting for Prue to arrive. Would she keep her promise and show up? And if so, what would they talk about? How could he break the ice so they both felt comfortable? He didn't even know what kind of coffee she drank so he couldn't preorder. Once she was there he would offer to buy her whatever she liked. He checked his watch again. 9:45. Fifteen minutes. He swallowed the knot of nerves lodged in his throat. This was the moment he'd been waiting for for the past five years and he was nervous. He didn't want to mess it up. He needed to know if there was a chance they could be together. He licked his dry lips and took a sip of his cold coffee then pushed the mug aside. What if she didn't show?

Nicholas thought back to the night of the charity auction. Prue had looked stunning in the dress she had worn with her hair up. She was a beautiful woman and he wanted her in his life. How could he make that happen? It occurred to him that she might be married. What then? He'd have no hope of ever being with her. Was she married? Was the man Nicholas had seen her with her husband?

He would have to wait to find out. He checked his watch for the third time. 9:50. *She'll be here any minute.*

♥

Prue drove along Fifth Avenue looking for a parking spot and as she cruised past the café she noticed Nicholas sitting at a table near the window. Her stomach did a nervous flip and she almost ran into the back of a parking car when her eyes left the road to look at the man she was about to have coffee with. She hit the brakes and berated herself for not being mindful of the traffic. The last thing she needed was to damage her mother's brand new car.

Turning down a side street, she spotted a Chrysler hatchback pulling out from the curb a car length away.

Prue gave a silent thank you and slipped into the space. She turned off the engine and sat. Her stomach felt as though a swarm of butterflies were flapping inside her. She took a deep breath, blew it out, pulled the keys from the ignition and opened the door. Today could define the rest of her life. Was she being too dramatic? She didn't think so.

Prue walked along the sidewalk and out onto Fifth Avenue. The café was across the street. As she got closer to the front entrance her breathing quickened, her heart raced and her palms grew sweaty. How long had Nicholas been waiting? Prue stopped and took a deep breath to force air into her lungs. She pulled the cap off her head and stuffed it into her purse, then ran her fingers through her curls. Toby was right, she had to do this for her own peace of mind.

She opened the door and the warmth of the coffee shop wrapped itself around her as she stepped inside out of the freezing cold. It was comforting.

When Nicholas saw her he stood up. Prue joined him at the table and they both took their seats.

"How are you?" He was happy she was there at last.

"I'm good. You?" She removed her gloves and sat her purse on the chair beside her.

"I'm good too." He smiled. "I'm glad you're here. Can I offer you a coffee or would you prefer to catch your breath first?" He couldn't take his eyes off her.

"Um, a vanilla latte would be nice. Thanks."

Nicholas left his seat to order the coffee. While waiting in the queue he kept checking to make sure Prue was still at their table. He had the distinct feeling she wanted to get up and run out of the café. How could he relieve her fears? Why was she afraid of him?

He placed the order and rejoined her. "I just needed to talk to you. I'm not here to make you uncomfortable."

"I – I know. But I'm not sure what you expect from this meeting." Prue glanced out of the window before returning her gaze to him. He was so handsome and seemed so unsure of himself right now.

"I wanted to see you again. I had hoped you'd want to see me too. Is there anything you want to know about me? There's so much I want to know about you." He realized he was overwhelming her with his questions. "I'm sorry. I'd just like to get to know you."

Prue fidgeted with her gloves. "Why?"

"I told you that the night of the charity auction."

Her cheeks grew warm. "I remember."

"Are you married? Is there someone in your life?"

Prue was taken aback by the forthrightness of his question. Should she let him think Toby was her man (because she assumed he already did) or should she tell him the truth? The thought circled her mind for a moment. "No, I'm not married. But…"

Nicholas' face fell. "You have someone in your life."

Their coffee arrived and they waited for the attendant to leave before continuing. "Thank you," Nicholas said.

"I do have someone in my life, but it isn't a man."

Nicholas frowned. "Isn't the man I saw you with…?"

She shook her head. "He's my brother, Toby."

"Your brother?" A huge weight lifted from his heart.

Prue nodded. Was she about to make the biggest mistake of her life?

"I'm confused." Then it occurred to him. If not a man was she saying a woman? Is that what she had meant the night of the benefit when she'd told him they were different people now? He hoped not.

She sighed and glanced down at the gloves in her hand. "I have a daughter."

"Oh." Nicholas sat back in his seat and attempted to digest the information she had revealed to him.

Twenty eight

Prue could see the confusion in Nicholas' eyes and she wondered what was going through his mind. She hadn't planned to tell him anything at all, but being with him and seeing him again brought the feelings she had held in her heart flooding back. He was her daughter's father and she was in love with him, despite her fear of what could happen. Would this whole situation turn around and become something wonderful? She was about to find out.

"So you were married?"

Prue shook her head. "Engaged to be married, but he… he died."

Nicholas gave her a sympathetic frown and reached for her hand. "I'm sorry."

A tear slid down Prue's cheek and she brushed it

away. "Thank you. It was a long time ago," she whispered unable to steady her voice.

"I lost my wife to a brain tumor," he told her, knowing what Prue had been through.

Prue's head snapped up and she stared into his eyes. "That must have been terrible for you."

Nicholas sighed. "It was. I thought I'd die too. It took a long time to… well you never really get over it, do you?" He gave a thin smile.

"No, you never do. But the pain gets easier to bear. Some of the time." She attempted to smile.

"Yes." He wanted to ask what had happened to her fiancé but wasn't sure he should.

"Do you have children?" Prue wanted to know.

He shook his head. "We wanted them. A houseful. But when Pam got sick she wasn't able to carry a child. Chemo and radiation treatments, you know? And she lost a lot of weight so her body wouldn't have coped."

Prue's eyes stung as she fought back tears. He had been through so much. So had she. She understood now why they had met that night. Both of them had suffered such an enormous personal loss. Did the universe bring people like them together on purpose? She wanted to believe it did.

She squeezed his hand, a pained expression on her face. "I'm so sorry."

He gave a thin smile. "Thanks. I appreciate it. But you've been through as much as I have. Can I ask how he died? You don't have to tell me if you don't want to."

Prue gave a heavy sigh. "Connor was partners with my brother in The Black Stallion Ranch and he'd gone on a stock run in the Cessna Cargomaster. When he couldn't be reached by radio Toby knew something was wrong, so he contacted the Emergency Services and gave a rough location of where the plane would have been if it had had to make a forced landing. When they went out there they found the wreckage. The plane had erupted into flames and…"

"Dear God," Nicholas said, squeezing her hand even tighter. "How horrible."

Prue's voice gave way. "Yes, it was." She took a breath to steady herself. "We were… childhood sweethearts and friends long before that. He was my whole world. I thought I would never recover and even though Connor was Toby's best friend, and Tobe was grieving too, my brother was my rock during those two and half years that I wanted to give up and die. He never left my side. That's why we're so close."

"That's understandable given the circumstances." He took a sip of his coffee and attempted to lighten the mood. "So tell me about your daughter."

Prue swallowed hard. This was it. The moment she'd been dreading for the past five years. No turning back. "Before I do there's something you should know."

Nicholas' eyebrows rose. "What is it?"

She cleared her throat. "This isn't easy for me. I – I never thought I'd be having this conversation with you. In fact I never thought we'd see each other again. Ever. I had no way to find you and…"

Nicholas eased his hand out of hers and rested it on her arm. "What are you trying to say?"

"Nick." Prue hesitated and licked her lips. "You're my daughter's father." She waited for his reaction, her heart beating twice as fast.

His eyes glazed over as though he were in shock. He didn't look at her, his mind was somewhere else.

Nicholas' mind replayed that night. Their gentle foreplay, her explosive climax and his eagerness to… *Oh God, I didn't use protection!* In the heat of passion neither of them had considered it. And he hadn't given it any thought afterward because their night together had been too perfect. *So it's true. I have a daughter.*

Prue placed her hand on his. "Nicholas? Nick? Talk to me."

A long sigh escaped his lips. He felt like he'd walked into a brick wall. "I have a daughter." It wasn't a question.

Prue glanced down at the table then returned her gaze to him. "Yes. You do. Like I said, I had no way of finding you. I didn't know your name or where you lived or any of that. Please don't be angry with me."

"I'm... I don't know what I am right now." He stared into her eyes as his became coherent. "She'd be five, right?"

She nodded and bit her bottom lip.

"What's her name?"

"Nicole. I thought..."

"Does she look like me?"

Prue nodded again and opened her purse. "I have a picture if you..."

"Why didn't you try to find me?"

Prue's dream popped into her head. This scenario was almost identical except they were in a public place. "How, Nick? How was I supposed to find you without any information? Did you try to find me?"

"Yes, as a matter of fact that's all I've been doing for the past five years." His voice was tight.

Prue could see irritation in his eyes. "If I'd known where to start I would have. Believe me I wanted to."

"Did you? Wasn't it easier to raise her on your own without any complications from me?"

Her breath caught in her throat. "That's not it at all." Although deep down Prue knew that was part of the reason.

Nicholas pushed back his chair and stood up. "I have to go."

Prue popped up out of her seat. "Please don't leave. Let's talk about this. Don't you want to meet her? She wants to meet you."

His angry eyes focused on her. "She knows about me?"

"Well, no, not exactly. She knows she has a daddy, of course, but she doesn't know it's you." She touched his arm, he pulled away. "Please, Nick, don't leave angry. I want to tell you about her."

"Give me your number. I need some time to make sense of all this." He was in love with a woman who had raised his daughter without him. How could he forgive her for that?

Prue took a pen from her purse and scribbled her cell number onto a napkin and handed it to him. "I'm sure we can work this out when you've had time to think about it. Please don't do anything rash."

"I'm not going to do anything for the moment." He brushed past Prue without looking at her and said, "I'll be in touch."

Prue eased her trembling body onto her seat, tears welling in her eyes, and realized she *had* made the biggest mistake of her life.

Twenty nine

When Prue arrived back at her parents' home Toby was on the front porch leaning against the railing waiting for her. He could see she was upset as she climbed the steps. Her face was flushed and her eyes red rimmed. He pulled her into his arms and asked what happened. She couldn't speak. Toby walked her along the porch and sat her in a wicker chair. "I'll be right back."

Prue rummaged through her purse for a tissue. She couldn't go inside looking the way she did. She had to blow her nose and freshen up her makeup.

Her brother returned with a shot of scotch. "Here, drink this."

She shook her head. "I'll be fine. I just need a minute to fix my face before I go into the house. I don't want mom to see me like this otherwise there's bound to be questions I don't feel up to answering right now. And if Nikki sees me she'll be worried too."

"Want to tell your big brother what happened?" Toby sat down.

Prue gave a heavy sigh. "I told him and he didn't take it well."

Toby's eyebrows rose. "You told him about Nikki?"

She nodded.

"What did he say?"

"He accused me of not making any effort to find him and wanting to raise Nikki on my own, then he took my number and said he'd be in touch." She turned her head and stared into her brother's eyes. "You don't think he meant his lawyer would be in touch do you?"

Toby frowned and wrapped an arm around her shoulders. "I don't know, sweetheart. I hope not." He wished he hadn't encouraged her to talk to the author. Everything his sister believed was coming true. "He needs time to think things through, that's all. Once he does he'll call."

Prue gave her brother a doubtful look. "I'm not so sure. He was pretty angry. The nice Nicholas I was having coffee with turned into someone completely different in a matter of minutes."

Toby pulled her closer and rested his chin on the top of her head. "I'm sorry you had to go through that. I wish I hadn't suggested you go when you wanted to cancel."

"It's not your fault, Tobe. I'm a grown woman. The decision was mine and I made it."

She pulled her makeup bag out of her purse and freshened up her face. "There, that looks better." She sniffled. "Ok. I'm ready to go in."

Nikki ran up to Prue the minute she walked through the door. "I missed you, Mommy."

Prue scooped her daughter into her arms. "I missed you too, sweetie pie."

"Grandma's making lunch. She's cooking a big lasagna for all of us. Smells good, huh? I'm so hungry."

Prue popped her little girl down on the entry hall rug. "Why not ask Grandma for a cookie to tide you over?"

Nikki pouted. "I already did but she said it would spoil my lunch."

"She used that one on us too. Wait here." Prue headed to the kitchen and within a minute was back with a chocolate chip cookie in her hand. "It's our secret, ok?"

"Thank you, Mommy." The little girl's eyes lit up. She took the cookie and ran off to the living room to watch the television.

"You rebel." Toby smirked and wagged a finger at her.

"Yep. That's me." Prue went upstairs to change.

When she reached the top landing tears stung the backs of her eyes and she blinked to keep them from spilling down her face. She walked along the hall, stepped into her room and closed the door and that's when they poured down her cheeks. She had opened Pandora's Box and now there was no way to close it. What would Nicholas do once he had time to think about it? Would he seek legal advice? Would he sue for custody? She had no idea what kind of man he truly was. She had put her trust in the man she thought him to be but had it all blown up in her face?

❦

Nicholas pulled his dad's four wheel drive into the driveway and climbed out. He had driven back to his parents' house on auto pilot thinking about everything he and Prue had discussed, especially the part about him having a five year old daughter he never knew existed. He felt a pang of guilt for being so harsh with Prue, but he had been thrown for a loop by her confession. Why hadn't she tried harder to find him? He had missed so much of his little girl's life. Time he could never get back, time he could have had getting to know her… to love her. He had always wanted kids. His heart ached.

When he stepped onto the front porch his sister came out the door shrugging into her jacket. "How'd it go?"

Nicholas frowned. "I don't want to talk about it."

Connie had witnessed the excitement in his eyes when he'd been getting ready to leave for his coffee date with Prue, now all she could see was hostility. "What happened?"

"I said I don't want to talk about it. Can you please leave it alone for now?" He headed for the front door.

"Wait a minute."

Nicholas swung around, his irritated gaze resting on his sister. "Please, Con, not now."

Connie sighed and raised her hands. "Ok. But when?"

"Later. Much later." He pushed the door open and stalked inside.

❧♥❧

Prue awoke to a knock on her bedroom door and realized she had dozed off instead of changing her clothes. She had been exhausted when she arrived home so it wasn't any wonder. The door opened and her mother peered inside.

"Lunch is ready, honey. I made your favorite. Lasagna."

Prue stretched and sat up. "Thanks, Mom. I'll change and be right down."

Her mother studied her for a moment. "Everything ok, honey?"

She nodded. "Everything's fine. I won't be long."

"Ok." Lorraine closed the door and stood in the hallway. Despite her daughter's confirmation that nothing was wrong she felt something was bothering Prue. As much as she wanted to know what it was she wouldn't pry. Prue would tell her in her own good time.

After lunch Nikki laid down for a nap on the sofa. Toby stretched out on the floor and Prue's mom and dad went out back to gather more fire wood. Prue sat down in an armchair and watched her daughter sleeping. She was an angel and she loved her with all her heart. *What happens if things get ugly? What happens if Nicholas wants sole custody of our daughter? He couldn't do that could he? Would he?* Prue had so many questions and no answers. Perhaps it was time to get legal counsel.

Rachelle would be able to recommend a good New York lawyer. When Prue got home after the New Year came in she'd talk to her friend about who could offer her the best advice. Better to be prepared.

Thirty

Two weeks into the New Year Prue was back at work. Rachelle was still on vacation for another couple of weeks as her show didn't recommence until the end of the month, but administration staff were required to do all the preliminary preparation before the new season began. Prue wanted to talk to her friend, tell her what had happened with Nicholas and ask about a good lawyer. Gabe came up to her office door and poked his head around. "Hi, lovely, have a nice weekend?"

Prue nodded. "Yep. What about you?"

Her colleague stepped into the room. "Quiet. But I like quiet sometimes."

"Mm, me too."

"Want to take in a movie Friday night? There's a new thriller on offer, now what was its name?" He brought his hand up to his chin and thought for a moment. "Oh well, anyway it sounds great. How about it?"

For the past few weeks, Prue had been so preoccupied with wondering when Nicholas would call that she hadn't been anywhere and was sure a night out would do her a world of good. "Thanks, I'd love to go."

"Cool. I'll organize the tickets. Do you want to go the whole hog and have dinner first?"

"Why not. Sounds like a fun night."

"Excellent. Looking forward to it." Gabe turned on his heel and marched down the corridor.

Prue sat and stared at her cell phone. Why hadn't Nicholas called? What was he planning? She sighed and willed the phone to ring. And it did, causing her to almost jump out of her skin. She snatched it off her desk not recognizing the number. "H – Hello?"

"Miss Prue Granger?" the male voice asked.

"Yes. Who's this?" Her stomach did an uneasy flip flop.

"My name is Benjamin Newman of Fitzgerald, Newman and Sayer law firm. I've been instructed to meet with you concerning a legal matter that has recently come across my desk. Can I make a time for you to come into our office?"

Her heart was ready to leap out of her throat. Prue couldn't breathe and she felt light-headed. Nicholas had hired lawyers. She sucked in a strangled breath and opened her mouth to speak but nothing came out. She cleared her throat. "Uh... I beg your pardon?"

"Miss Granger I need to meet with you. This is time sensitive so the sooner you can come into the office the better. I need certain information from you before we can proceed."

Prue's heart hammered so hard she thought it would explode in her chest. "Um, I – I guess so. Can you tell me what it's about?"

"I'd prefer to discuss the matter with you in person. How does tomorrow at two sound?"

"I – I'll have to check with my manager first."

"Why don't I pencil you in and if there's a problem you can contact our office to reschedule."

"Oh, ok." Prue's body was trembling. "Would you give me your number please?"

Benjamin provided Prue with the relevant details and, before ringing off, told her he looked forward to meeting with her the next afternoon.

Prue sat dazed. She couldn't believe it. Nicholas was going to try to gain custody of her daughter.

Anger outweighed anxiety and Prue whipped her phone off the desk and keyed in Nicholas' number. He wouldn't get away with it. The call went to voicemail and Prue didn't leave a message. Of course he wouldn't talk to her now.

She pressed speed dial and called Toby.

"Hello, Black Stallion Ranch…"

"Tobe, it's me."

"Hey, sis, I was just thinking about you."

"Nicholas hired a lawyer. He was just on the phone with me making an appointment to meet with him tomorrow afternoon."

"That sonofabitch! I'll be there in a few hours."

"What? No. You can't drive all this way. I'll be fine."

"I want to be there with you when you speak to the lawyer. Why would Nicholas do something like this without talking to you first?"

Prue rested her head in her hand. "I don't know. I guess he's decided a court battle will give him the results he wants. Why would he bother telling me about it? Talk about blindsided. He has all the resources to win, Tobe. I don't."

Toby sighed. "Look, I'm coming across. I should be there by seven. We'll talk about it then."

"Thanks, Tobe. I didn't expect you to come all this way, but I'm glad you are."

"Where else could I be."

"Please don't say anything to mom and dad. I don't want them involved in any of this."

"I won't. I have to go pack. See you later."

"Ok." Prue pushed her cell onto the desk. Now she knew why Nicholas hadn't called.

She didn't much feel like going out at the end of the week. All of a sudden her world had come crashing down around her and all she wanted to do was take her daughter and disappear. How could she have been so stupid to even think Nicholas would be decent about the whole situation? As she had said before, nice men do nasty things and he had proved that.

Thirty one

The next afternoon Prue and Toby sat in the sophisticated foyer of Fitzgerald, Newman and Sayer waiting to meet with Benjamin Newman. The law firm's office was on the 11th floor of a modern high-rise overlooking Third Avenue. Prue fidgeted with her hands while she waited, nervous about the meeting. Would Nicholas attend? She hoped not. As far as she was concerned she never wanted to lay eyes on him again. She had suspected this would happen. Why had she been so foolish to tell him about their daughter? Why had she placed her trust in a man she didn't really know?

The attractive, young brunette at the reception desk replaced the telephone receiver, looked over at Prue and smiled. "Mr. Newman will see you now. Just down the hall, second door on the left."

Prue and her brother stood up, glanced at each other and headed along the hallway. When they reached the door with Benjamin Newman's name on it the door opened. "Good afternoon, Miss Granger. Nice to meet you." The lawyer held out his hand.

Prue shook it. "Good to meet you too, Mr. Newman."

Benjamin eyed the tall man standing beside Prue.

She glanced at Toby. "This is my brother, Tobias. He wanted to be with me today. That's alright, isn't it?"

The lawyer held out his hand. "Of course it is. Good to meet you, Tobias."

"Please, call me Toby." He shook hands.

They entered the office and Benjamin offered them each a seat in front of his desk. He moved around to his expensive, leather executive chair and sat down, picking up a pair of spectacles and placing them on his nose before opening the file in front of him.

Prue watched him with nervous eyes, wringing her hands. "What's this all about, Mr. Newman?"

Benjamin glanced up from the paperwork in his hand and smiled. "Well, Miss Granger, I've been instructed by Mr. Nicholas Colton to…"

"So this is about my daughter, Nikki?"

"Yes." He motioned to the documents. "May I?"

Prue nodded. "Of course," she said, her voice quiet.

"Mr. Colton has instructed our office to set up a trust fund for his daughter, Nicole Granger."

Prue and Toby gaped at each other.

"I'll need details of your daughter's full name, date of birth and other necessary information to finalize the account for her. And a copy of her birth certificate. You can provide that today, can't you?"

Prue was speechless. She nodded. She'd brought along copies of Nikki's documents just in case.

"Good. Mr. Colton has appointed $500.000 for any medical, educational and college expenses required now and in the future. Of course in the next sixteen years this sum will grow substantially and by the time it has matured your daughter should have over one million dollars in the account. In the interim, should she require any medical, dental or other expenses covered in the trust fund provisions that can be arranged through our office. You only need to contact us and provide original invoices. Nicole will be able to access the remainder of these funds when she reaches the age of twenty one. Clear so far?"

Again Prue nodded.

"Alright." He passed a questionnaire across the desk to her. "If you could complete this while I step out of the office for a moment we'll get the account in motion today." Benjamin stood up and left the room.

Prue glanced at her brother sideways. "I was sure this was a custody meeting. I never dreamed he'd do something like this. Five hundred thousand dollars? Toby that's incredible!"

"You're not kidding. Nikki's set for the rest of her life. And you don't have to worry about where the money's coming from for her education, college... anything."

"I can't believe it. Pinch me so I know I'm not dreaming."

"You're not dreaming. This is real."

Prue studied the paper in front of her. Standard information. She picked up the pen and filled it out.

"How can I thank him when he won't talk to me?"

Toby rested a reassuring hand on her arm. "Give him time. I think he'll come around."

"I hope you're right."

Benjamin returned to the office. "All done?"

"Yes." Prue passed the document to the lawyer.

"Great. Once the trust fund has been set up, which should take about a week, the money can be accessed for the specified necessities. We'll file a copy with the state and mail a copy to you in the next week or two, so you can peruse the documents at your leisure to get a better understanding of the requirements of a trust fund. Please read them carefully. That's it. Pretty painless." He smiled.

Prue and Toby stood up. "Thank you so much, Mr. Newman. It wasn't at all what I expected." She held out her hand.

Benjamin shook it. "You're welcome, Miss Granger." He turned to Toby and shook his hand. "Mr. Granger. It's been a pleasure meeting you both. Take care now."

In the elevator on the way down, Prue needed to take a minute to get her head around what had just happened. She thought today would be the end of her world as she knew it but Nicholas had surprised her with his generous gift to Nikki. She had to thank him. Somehow.

$\mathcal{T}$hirty two

Nicholas sat on the front porch of his Monterey cliffside home, gazing out at the foamy waves rolling into shore. The sky had turned charcoal gray, a sure indication that rain was on the way. His best friend, Peter Moncrieff, would arrive any minute with an extra-large pizza and a six pack of beer. They were sharing take out and watching a marathon run of the Die Hard movies, all six of them if they could manage it. It was Friday so Nicholas could afford a late night of entertainment for once.

He had to do something to take his mind off his current circumstances. Not that he could. He had a daughter. A little princess. It elated and scared him at the same time. She didn't know him and he didn't know her and may never get to. He wondered what she was like.

Nicholas wasn't sure he could face Prue again. He felt betrayed and it outweighed the love he held in his heart for her. Setting up the trust fund for his daughter was the best he could offer right now. He pulled himself out of the porch chair, headed for the door and stepped into the house. His friend had just pulled into the drive.

Peter waltzed through the front door carrying the over-sized pizza box, a six pack of beer and a large packet of potato crisps. "Hey, pal, ready to get into Die Hard with a vengeance?" He grinned and wriggled his eyebrows.

"Ha, ha, very funny," Nicholas said with an unamused chuckle.

"Yeah, I thought so." Peter stood the beer on the coffee table and set the pizza box down. He dropped the bag of potato crisps on the floor next to the table leg and took a seat on the sofa. "So start the movie already, I'm starved."

"Ok. Ok. Keep your shirt on." Nicholas picked up the remote control and switched on his 85" high definition smart TV. The Blu-ray disc was in the player ready to go. He sat down next to his friend and was about to hit PLAY when Peter spoke.

"So when are you going to cut the girl some slack and go talk to her?"

Nicholas gave him a sideward glance and sat the remote on the coffee table. "It's not that simple."

"Sure it is." His friend turned to face him, resting his elbow on the back of the sofa. "Be honest with yourself, Nick. You couldn't find her so how was she supposed to find you? Why are you being so hard on her?"

"Because in the end I did find her." He folded his arms. "And she could have found me if she'd tried."

"You're a well-connected author with certain resources." Peter pointed at himself. "She didn't have those advantages."

"Ok. Fair enough. But she could have at least made some effort."

Peter gave him an incredulous frown. "How do you know she didn't?"

"Because she volunteered that information." Nicholas flipped open the cardboard carton and stared at the massive pepperoni pizza. The conversation had diminished his appetite and he sighed.

"You know you're not being fair, don't you?"

"I can't help how I feel, Pete."

Peter folded his arms. "Well maybe you should try. You have a little girl out there who wants to meet you. Don't you want to meet her?"

Nicholas frowned. "Of course I do." He gave a frustrated huff. "Look, I don't need psychoanalyzing. Are we watching the movie or not?"

His friend sighed. "Yeah, yeah, we're watching the movie. I think you're making a huge mistake, though. But don't take my word for it. Just remember, if you leave it too long it might be too late." He pulled a beer from the pack, twisted the cap and took a generous swig.

Forty five minutes into the first Die Hard instalment Nicholas couldn't concentrate on the movie. His mind was conflicted over what to do about the unfamiliar situation he had found himself in. Deep down, he knew Pete was right. He should get over himself and call Prue, but something inside him wouldn't allow him to. Maybe it was pride.

"Argh, Alan Rickman's character is such an asshole in this movie," Pete remarked, taking a bite of his left over pizza slice. "I wish someone would shoot him already."

Nicholas' mind snapped back to the present and he gazed at the TV screen, but didn't make comment because he hadn't been paying attention. He sighed and bit into the cold piece of pizza in his hand. No matter how hard he tried he couldn't get Prue or his little girl out of his mind.

♥

The next morning, Nicholas was at his desk sitting in front of his laptop frowning at the blank white page staring back at him from the computer screen. The day was gray with heavy, charcoal colored clouds hanging low in the sky. Rain just beginning to fall pattered against the window panes of his office and a chill crept into the air around him. It was perfect writing weather, but for some reason his muse had gone on vacation. Maybe she was mad at him too for not acting like an adult and facing the situation with Prue head on.

What was he supposed to do? There were always consequences: for every action there was a reaction. And his reaction had been justified. She had hurt him and he didn't think he could forgive her or pretend everything was alright when it wasn't. Was he being sanctimonious? He had inadvertently gotten her pregnant to begin with, so he should accept some of the responsibility.

Nicholas gave a heavy sigh and typed the title of his next blockbuster novel onto the blank page. He had a six month deadline and had to keep focused or the book wouldn't be completed in time. The situation with Prue would have to take a back seat. Would he ever call her with the offer to negotiate a suitable arrangement where their daughter was concerned? He didn't have any answers.

❧ ♥ ❧

A knock on her front door pulled Prue out of her daze. She had been thinking about Nicholas all morning and as she stepped into the entry hall she wondered if it was him standing outside her apartment ready to talk. She peered into the peephole, caught sight of the golden locks and threw the door open. "Rachelle. It's so good to see you!" She gave her friend a tight hug.

"It's good to see you, too." Rachelle stepped into the hall, slipped out of her jacket and hung it on the coat rail beside the door. "I come bearing gifts." She held up a shopping bag.

Nikki rushed out of her room and ran along the hall. "Aunty Rachelle, you're back." She reached her arms up to give the woman a hug.

"I am, sweetie, and I have presents from Santa. He dropped these off at my place while I was away."

Nikki clapped her hands. "I love presents."

They stepped into the living room and sat down on the sofa. Rachelle pulled the presents out of the bag and handed them around.

"Ok. This is for you." She passed a colorful package to Nikki. "And this is for you." She passed a medium-sized, gold-wrapped box to Prue."

Nikki ripped the wrapping off her gift. "Yay! Minions. Thank you, Aunty Rachelle." She turned to her mother. "Can I watch it now, Mommy?"

Prue took the Blu-ray from her daughter's hand. "Sure, honey. Want to sit on the floor over there?"

Nikki positioned herself center to the television screen and waited for the movie to begin.

Returning to her seat, Prue picked up the present Rachelle had given her and unwrapped it. A white Pandora box. She flipped it open. Inside sat a beautiful silver bracelet with three charms: a little girl, a cloud's silver lining, and best friends. A tear slipped down Prue's cheek and she hugged her friend. "Thank you. It's lovely."

"I wanted you to know that I'm here for you." She balled all of the wrapping up and dropped it into the shopping bag. "So, tell me, how was Christmas?"

Prue gave her a serious gaze. "A lot happened over the holidays but I can't say too much right now." She motioned to Nikki with a nod of her head.

Rachelle's right eyebrow arched. "Does it have anything to do with a certain author?"

Prue nodded.

Her friend's eyes widened. "Damn, now I'm so curious I could burst."

"Sorry." Prue stood up. "Want some coffee?"

Rachelle sighed. "Coffee sounds good."

"I have some homemade cookies too."

"Yum." Rachelle moved to the dining table and took a seat near the window.

Prue returned to the living room with the mugs of coffee and a plate of cookies and took her seat. "I can tell you a little about what happened." She glanced at her daughter who was engrossed in the movie and giggling with glee. "His family lives in Kennedy, only twenty minutes or so out of Downtown Pittsburgh. We ran into each other at the supermarket on Christmas Eve, of all places."

"What?"

Prue nodded. "He asked if we could meet for coffee and I agreed."

"What happened when you met?"

"We talked for a bit. He told me his wife died from a brain tumor. I told him about Connor."

"Poor man." She rested a hand on Prue's arm. "Poor you, too. You've both been through so much tragedy."

"It was all going so well until I told him." Prue sipped her coffee, waiting for her friend's reaction.

Rachelle's mouth gaped, then she whispered, "You told him about..." She motioned at Nikki with her eyes.

Prue nodded.

"What did he say?"

"He didn't take it well. He got angry and left and I haven't heard from him since."

"OMG!" She sipped her coffee. "Anything else?"

"He set up a five hundred thousand dollar trust fund for her."

Rachelle almost choked on her coffee. "Jiminy Cricket. I told you he wasn't a deadbeat dad."

Prue sighed. "I know. I want to thank him but he won't answer my calls. Do you have any idea where he lives?"

"We already know he lives in Monterey by his author bio. Let me see what I can dig up and I'll call you when I find out something."

"Thanks, Rachelle. I really appreciate your help."

"What are friends for?" She took another sip of coffee. "Wow. A lot did happen over the holidays, didn't it?"

"Yep. You could say that."

Thirty three

Rachelle called Prue Sunday evening to tell her she had Nicholas' address. She told Prue he owned a cliffside cottage overlooking the Monterey Peninsula tourist route and had been living there for the past several years. She suggested Prue take some sick leave (as she had a week up her sleeve) and travel to California to see the author and try to talk things through.

Prue thought it was a great idea, but wondered what would happen if management found out she was away rather than at home tucked up in bed with the flu? Rachelle said she would cover for her, that she knew a GP who could provide a doctor's certificate, and for Prue to organize a flight right away. No time like the present.

Before she had time to change her mind Prue booked a direct flight for seven the next morning, with the plane arriving in Monterey at around ten o'clock California time, and also pre-booked a cab to take her to JFK Airport. Her accommodation reservation was also arranged.

She hoped she was doing the right thing.

Prue organized clothes for Nikki to take to Yolanda's, her favorite toys and some snacks. She then set to work packing her own suitcase. She wasn't sure how long she'd be away so she packed enough clothing for the week.

Nikki was always excited about staying over with her friend Jacinta and tonight was no exception. She grabbed the handle of her case and wheeled it along the hall to her friend's apartment, Prue close behind her, and knocked on the door. Yolanda opened it and Nikki kissed her mom goodbye and ran inside to play with Jacinta.

"Thank you so much for doing this on such short notice," Prue said. "I don't know how I can thank you enough for the many times you've watched Nikki for me."

Yolanda waved the comment off. "Hey, I don't mind. You've done the same for me and Jazz loves having Nikki here, so do we. She's no trouble. So no thanks necessary."

Prue gave Yolanda a tight hug. "You're the best. I hope you know that?"

"Duane keeps telling me I am, so I better believe it." She chuckled.

"I'll call you once I'm settled in at the inn."

"Ok. Safe journey."

"Thank you." Prue headed back to her apartment to organize herself.

❦

When the flight touched down at Monterey Airport Prue's stomach flipped over. She was on Nicholas' home turf. What would he say when she showed up at his home? Would he be happy to see her or would he still be angry? She had to see him, had to thank him for his generous gift to their daughter. She hoped he'd be pleased to find her standing at his door. And she hoped he'd want to talk.

After collecting her suitcase, Prue headed outside to the pickup point to find a cab. She noticed a sign for Hertz rentals and decided to hire a car instead. It would make traveling from place to place that much easier.

She had booked a room in Pacific Grove at Gosby House Inn, a charming two-story Victorian on Lighthouse Avenue not far from the city center, and was looking forward to getting settled in before making the trip out to Nicholas' home. The pictures she had viewed online of the quaint guest house rooms looked beautiful, like stepping back in time, and she knew she'd enjoy her stay.

Once in the hire car, Prue set the GPS and drove out of the airport. It would take around eighteen minutes to get to the inn.

Prue pulled into a vertical car space out front of the yellow and white mansion and sat gazing up at the gorgeous, bygone era home with its steepled roof and stained glass window panes. Her heart did a happy dance. How lovely the place was. She breathed a contented sigh, stepped out of the hatchback and grabbed her suitcase from the trunk. The Monterey Peninsula was simply breathtaking and Prue planned to do some sightseeing while she was there.

She climbed the nine red brick steps to the small front porch and entered the building.

ॐ♥ॐ

As Prue pulled into the steep driveway her throat tightened. Was she making another huge mistake? She turned off the engine and sat for a moment, her stomach doing jittery flip flops beneath her belt. She gazed at her reflection in the rearview mirror. "Are you doing the right thing, Prue," she asked herself.

She gave a heavy sigh, pulled the keys from the ignition and stepped out of the rental. *I'm here so I may as well get it over with.* She climbed the fifteen wooden steps set into the side of the cliff and stepped onto the porch. The view was spectacular. Her hand shook as she raised it to knock and she drew back. Prue swallowed the nervous lump in her throat and rapped on the wood and glass door.

"Just a sec," a male voice called from inside.

Prue stepped back and waited for the door to open.

When it did she was surprised. The man wasn't Nicholas. "Hi, uh, I'm looking for Nicholas Colton. He does live here, doesn't he?"

Peter recognized her immediately. "Yeah, he does. He's away at the moment. I'm looking after his dogs." He glanced behind him as Rocky and Benji moved up close. "Sorry for being rude. I'm Peter." He held out his hand. Now he could see why Nick was in love with the woman. She was stunning, and the mother of his child.

Prue shook his hand. "I'm Prue. Can you tell me when he'll be back?"

"It's cold out there. Want some coffee?"

"Thanks, but I probably shouldn't." She gazed past him through the doorway.

"I don't think Nick'll mind, if that's what you're worried about. I just made a fresh pot and I can't drink it all."

"Ok, if you're sure."

Peter stepped aside and Prue entered the well-appointed home. "He has nice taste."

"Yeah, he does. Follow me." He moved through the living room to the kitchen. "Have a seat." Peter gestured to the breakfast table. "How do you take it?"

"Uh, black's fine. Thank you." She pulled the purple scarf from around her neck and shrugged out of her black wool jacket. "So you're the PI friend he told me about."

"That would be me, yes." He walked over and sat a mug in front of Prue then took a seat opposite and sipped his coffee.

"I guess Nick's told you about me, too."

"That would be another yes." He smiled.

Prue gave a thin smile.

Rocky and Benji came up to Prue, Rocky nudging her arm with his massive head.

"Seems the boys like you. They don't take to everyone, you know."

Prue gave each of them a pat. "Hi fella. Hey you." She glanced at Peter. "They're gorgeous animals. I've always had a soft spot for Rottweilers. They remind me of big, cuddly teddy bears." She rubbed under each of the dogs' chins.

Peter folded his arms and watched her for a moment. He gave a heavy sigh and said, "Prue, there's something you should know."

Thirty four

Nicholas stepped out of the cab and crossed the sidewalk to the revolving door of the broadcast center. He took a deep breath and pushed through the glass turnstile into the reception foyer. One of the ladies behind the counter recognized him. "Good morning, Mr. Colton. Good to see you again. What can I help you with?"

Taking a quick glance at the young woman's name tag he said, "Good morning, Rebecca, I'd like to speak to Prue Granger, if that's possible."

She smiled up at him. "Let me check for you." She called a number. "Hi, Mr. Colton is here to see Prue. Oh, ok. Yes, I'll tell him."

"I'm sorry, Mr. Colton, but Prue is on medical leave. Rachelle's on her way down."

"Thanks." He frowned as he moved away from the

front desk. Medical leave? He hoped she was alright and that it wasn't anything serious.

Rachelle rushed along the corridor and out into the lobby. Nicholas was standing off to the side waiting for her. She held out her hand to him as she approached. "Nick, good to see you again."

He shook her hand. "Good to see you too, Rachelle. A belated Happy New Year."

"Yes, and the same to you." She took his arm and they moved to the front of the foyer.

"I hear Prue's sick. Nothing serious, I hope."

Rachelle shook her head. "She's in Monterey. She went there to see you. And it appears you had the same idea."

Nicholas frowned. "She is? When did she leave?"

"This morning. I gather you left this morning as well. Great minds think alike, huh?" She smiled.

"Do you know where she's staying?"

"She's at a B&B in Pacific Grove called Gosby House Inn. Do you know it?"

He smiled. "As a matter of fact I do. Friends of mine manage the place."

"God, this is getting spookier by the minute. Serendipity is at work here, I'm sure of it."

Nicholas' left eyebrow rose. He'd been thinking the same thing. "Well I'd better try to get on the next flight out otherwise she might come up with the same idea and fly back."

"No, no. I'll give her a call and make sure she stays put."

"Thanks, Rachelle. I appreciate it."

"No problem at all. Please, just work it out! Ok?"

"I hope we can."

☙ ♥ ❧

Prue gaped at Peter. "Are you serious?" She couldn't believe Nicholas had done what she had and flown to New York to talk to her... and on the same day too.

"Couldn't be more serious." He sipped his coffee. "I dropped him at the airport this morning."

Prue huffed. "Huh, so what do I do now?" Her cell phone went off and her body jumped. She glanced at Peter and gave a nervous giggle as she fossicked through her purse for her phone. "H – Hello?"

"Hey, it's me. You'll never guess who I was talking to a few minutes ago," Rachelle asked.

"Nicholas?"

"How'd you know that?"

"I'm at his house. His friend, Peter, told me."

"Is his friend cute?"

Prue's gaze moved to the PI. "Somewhat. Why did you call?"

"To tell you to stay put. Nick's on his way back."

"Did he tell you to say that or…"

"I told him I'd call you and he thanked me, so that would be a yes."

"Ok. Is he coming home?"

"No. I think he's heading to the guest house."

Prue jumped out of her seat. "Oh. I'd better go then."

"You don't have to leave right away. Just make sure you're at the inn within six hours or so. The flight will take that long. Might be a good idea to pick the PI's brain about Nicholas. See if there's anything you should know."

"You think so?"

"It's the perfect opportunity to find out what you can, while you can. Why not?"

Prue glanced at Peter. "Maybe you're right. Thanks for letting me know. I'll talk to you later."

"Talk later. Good luck."

Prue dropped her phone into her purse. "My friend, Rachelle." She gave an awkward smile. "Nick's on his way back."

"That's good news. Maybe now you two can get things sorted." He leaned back on the chair and folded his arms.

"Yes, hopefully." Prue picked up her mug and sipped the coffee. "How long have you known each other?"

Peter scratched the back of his head. "Let me see. About… fifteen years, give or take. I was a cop with the LAPD before I became a PI. Nick was a lawyer back then."

Prue's eyebrows rose. "A lawyer?"

"Yeah, and a damn good one too." He rubbed the stubble on his chin.

"Wow. That's something I didn't know." She took another sip of coffee. "Criminal law, I take it?"

"You would be right. He was one of the good guys. He couldn't be bought off or threatened. He did the best he could to keep lowlifes off the streets."

"What made him give it up?"

He looked into her eyes and frowned. "You know about Pam?"

Prue nodded. "A little."

Peter sighed. "When she passed away Nick… well, he wasn't the same. He came to realize life was indeed too short and decided to throw it in and do what he loved. Not that he didn't love his job, he did, but I think he needed a distraction. Something to take him away from the reality of life without Pam."

Prue blinked back tears. "I can understand that," she said, her voice quiet.

He watched her for a moment. "Yeah. Nick told me about your fiancé. I'm sorry."

"It's been…" She thought for a moment, "eight years now. But thanks."

"Yeah, it's been about that for Nick too. Loss is hard. It takes a long time to get over." His eyes met hers. "But I guess you already know that. I'm not sure Nick is truly over losing Pam."

Prue stared at him. "What makes you say that?"

"Maybe the fact that he won't go to put flowers on her grave and things he says sometimes."

"What kind of things?"

Peter realized he'd spoken out of turn and gave Prue a thin smile. "Look, I shouldn't have said anything. You'd best talk to him about it."

Thirty five

Prue was on the small front porch waiting for Nicholas to arrive. He had messaged her to let her know he'd be at the inn around seven. The winter chill wrapped itself around her and she shivered, wondering if it was the night air or her nerves causing her body to react that way. Both, she realized. She was a long way from home and if things went badly she'd have no one there to comfort her and a long flight home alone.

She gave a heavy sigh and descended the steps to wait on the sidewalk. He would arrive at any minute and she didn't want him having to go into reception to ask for her.

A taxi pulled into the curb at the corner and Nicholas stepped out. He looked just as handsome as ever in his knee length, fawn wool coat and burgundy scarf. He stepped onto the sidewalk, walked over to Prue, leaned in and kissed her cheek. "How are you? Chilly night, isn't it."

Prue rested a hand on his arm to steady herself and took a deep breath. "I'm fine. Yes, it is chilly. Must be coming off the ocean."

"Must be." He smiled. "It's good to see you."

Prue wanted to say 'Is it?' but decided against it. "Good to see you, too."

"Have you eaten?" Nicholas took a pair of leather gloves from the pocket of his coat and pulled them on.

Prue shook her head.

"Me either. There's a great Thai place on the next corner." He pointed along the street. "Want to stroll over and have some dinner? You do like Thai, don't you?"

"Yes I do. That would be nice. Thank you."

"Great." He linked his arm through hers and they headed to the restaurant.

Prue felt as though she were dreaming. After everything that had happened, and Nicholas not wanting to speak to her, what had caused his sudden turn around? Had he finally come to his senses?

Once they were seated, Prue wanted to tell Nicholas how grateful she was for the generous trust fund he'd set up for their daughter, but wasn't sure if she should. Perhaps it would be better to wait and see where he steered the conversation before bringing anything up of that nature. Maybe he wanted to keep things light over dinner, preferring to discuss the more important topics later.

He glanced around the restaurant. "What do you think?"

"It has a lovely ambiance."

"Yes it does. I've eaten here many times and the food is great as well. I hope you like it."

Prue smiled. "I'm sure I will."

Nicholas' gaze remained on her and Prue's stomach did an uneasy flip flop. She picked up the glass in front of her and sipped the water.

"It's strange how we both decided to fly over at the same time to see each other, isn't it?"

She looked into his eyes. "Yes. Rachelle would say it's serendipity."

"Actually, she did."

Prue's eyes widened. "She said that to you?"

He nodded. "And, you know, I was thinking the same thing. Not that I believe in that fate stuff, but…" He shrugged.

"I'm not sure I do either, but who knows." She took another sip of water and cleared her throat. "Nick?"

His eyes were still on her. "Yes, Prue."

"I'd like to thank you for the trust fund you set up for Nikki. It's such a generous gift. I hope you know how grateful I am."

"It's the least I could do." He rested his elbows on the table, clasped his hands together and pressed his thumbs under his chin. "Tell me about her."

"What would you like to know?"

"Everything. Whatever you think is meaningful."

"Well… let me show you her picture first." Prue dug around her purse for her wallet. She opened it and slid the small photo from the plastic sleeve and passed it to him.

Nicholas took the photo and studied it. She looked exactly like him when he was young. Same eyes, same hair color, same dimple in the chin. He smiled. "She's lovely. A little princess." He passed the photo back.

Prue shook her head. "You keep it."

He pulled his wallet from his pants pocket and slipped the photo into the empty plastic sleeve. "Thank you."

"And yes, she is a little princess. She's smart and funny and… adorable. She loves to read too. I wanted her to appreciate books as much as I do."

"That's good. Reading opens up a whole new world and broadens the mind. My parents did the same for me. I think that's why I love writing and reading so much."

She hesitated for a moment. "Would… would you like to meet her?"

Nicholas clasped his hands in front of him. "At some point I would, yes, but not right now."

Prue frowned. "Why not?"

"You and I have a lot of talking to do. Who knows where it'll lead? I don't want to do anything that could hurt Nikki. I hope you understand."

Prue knew what he meant. He wasn't sure if he could forgive her for not telling him about his daughter. He wasn't sure if he wanted a life with them both. Why was he here then? To talk, he'd said. What about?

"I certainly don't want Nikki hurt either, but why are we here if you don't want to work things out?"

"I'm not saying…" The meals arrived and Nicholas waited to continue. "I'm not saying I don't want to work things out with you. All I'm saying is it will take time. And until we work it out I don't want to bring our daughter into it."

Prue set her knife and fork down. "Alright. That's fair, I guess." She was disappointed that Nicholas didn't want to meet his daughter, but knew he was right. If things didn't work out between them what would be the point of him being a part of Nikki's life if he didn't plan to stay.

She had hoped he would want to be in their little girl's life regardless of how it all turned out, but she had obviously been wrong about that and it hurt.

"Prue, I'm not trying to be difficult. Believe me. I don't want any of us to be hurt. And I do want to be a part of Nikki's life but we need to tread carefully where she's concerned. I…"

"I understand," Prue said in a quiet tone. Her heart ached at the thought of Nicholas walking out of their lives for good. Would he?

He reached across and squeezed her hand. "Don't be upset. Let's take it one day at a time. Ok?"

Prue nodded because she knew if she opened her mouth the tears stinging the backs of her eyes would spill. She was in love with this man and she knew he was in love with her but the timing seemed to be off once again.

After dinner, Nicholas and Prue strolled back to the inn, not arm in arm this time. The evening hadn't gone at all as she had expected. If he was so intent on flying to New York to see her why was he now saying he wasn't sure how things would turn out? At the steps to the inn, Nicholas pulled her into his arms and stared into her eyes. "Want a night cap?"

"I – It's getting late and I have to…"

He pressed his mouth to hers and Prue melted in his arms. When the kiss ended he eased her away from him and stepped back. "I'm sorry. I shouldn't have done that."

Prue looked at him with tear-filled eyes. "Why did you? You need to make up your mind if you want me in your life or not." She turned around and hurried up the steps.

"Prue. Wait." He moved up beside her. "Come home with me so we can talk in private. The restaurant wasn't the place to discuss our personal issues."

She frowned and brushed a tear from her cheek. "You mean now?"

"Yes. Now."

She sighed. "I don't…"

He leaned in and gazed into her eyes. "You want to work things out, don't you?"

"Of course I do."

He held out his hand. "Well then?"

"Alright." Prue blew out a frustrated breath and took his hand. "I have a rental over there." She pointed to the silver Nissan hatch.

"Why don't I drive? It'll be quicker that way."

She handed him the remote key. "Ok."

Although the winter night was cold, the sky had myriad twinkling stars. Cabrillo Highway was dark with very few cars and only the headlights guiding their way. Neither of them spoke as they drove the winding road to Nicholas' home and Prue wondered how they were going to talk things through if they didn't open their mouths. Would he be able to forgive her for something she'd had no control over? Her heart ached at the thought of not having him in her life. How could she convince him to stay?

Thirty six

Nicholas opened the front door to his home, turned on the lights and gestured for Prue to step in ahead of him. He closed the door, moved up behind her to help her out of her jacket and hung it on the coat rail in the entry hall. Once he'd removed his coat and scarf he ushered Prue into the living room and disappeared through an adjoining doorway. "Won't be a minute."

The house was warm, cozy and well-furnished.

Prue wandered over to the sofa, sat down, and gazed around the room. A well-stocked bookshelf lined one complete wall from ceiling to floor, another wall displayed two picture frames with what appeared to be an ancient manuscript page in each, and the credenza held numerous literary awards Nicholas had won.

"Can I offer you that nightcap now?" He came into the living room carrying two, long-stemmed crystal glasses and a bottle of expensive-looking French wine.

"Just a little, thanks," Prue said. She had no intention of getting drunk and making a complete fool of herself.

Nicholas set the glasses on the large, oak coffee table and opened the wine. "It's a 1990 Bordeaux Merlot." He poured a full glass for himself and half a glass for Prue then picked up hers and passed it to her. "I hope it's as good as they say."

Prue took a cautious sip. She didn't want to drink it too quickly because she knew it would go to her head. "Mm, it's good."

Nicholas took a large swallow and joined Prue on the sofa. "You're right, it is."

"Are they real?" Prue pointed to the manuscript pages on the wall opposite.

Nicholas shook his head and took another sip of wine. "I wish. No, they're copies. Shakespeare sonnets."

"Oh? Which ones?" She loved Shakespeare's poetry and plays.

"That one," he pointed to the left frame, "is Sonnet 18. Shall I compare thee to a summer's day."

"Thou art more lovely and more temperate. I love that one." Prue sipped more wine.

"You do?"

She nodded and continued to sip her wine.

"What about that one?" She pointed to the other frame.

"That one's rather morose. Sonnet 30. When to the sessions of sweet silent thought I summon up remembrance of things past."

"I know that one too. Not a favorite, but still a wonderful piece of writing."

He was impressed that Prue was a patron of the arts. She surprised him more every time he saw her, in one way or another.

He breathed a heavy sigh. "Look, Prue, I realize now that it was difficult for you to find me. As I mentioned to you that day at the café, I've been looking for you for the past five years and had no luck until Pete suggested doing a composite of your face. That's how we found you. His friend at the DMV ran your picture through their database and matched it to your driver's license."

"I would never have come up with that idea. I had thought about hiring a private investigator, but what would I have told him? I had nothing to offer." She sipped the wine. It was good. She sipped some more, the tension ebbing away, her shoulders relaxing.

"I know. And I'm sorry I was angry. It was stupid of

me." He took another generous mouthful of wine.

Prue continued to sip until her glass was empty.

Nicholas poured more wine into it. "I do want to be part of Nikki's life. I'd like to get to know her. So much time has passed already." He finished the last of his wine and refilled his glass.

"Yes it has." Prue swallowed a large mouthful of the Merlot then set her glass down on the coffee table and touched his face. "I'm truly sorry for that."

Nicholas sat his glass on the table, took her hand and kissed the palm.

Prue searched his eyes. She could see the love he had for her was still there. Was there hope? Could they be together?

He leaned in to her. "Prue, I…" His mouth was on hers, hungry, needing her.

She slid an arm around his neck and pulled him closer. His firm masculine body pressed to hers sent an expectant quiver to her belly. The heated kiss continued.

Nicholas pulled his mouth from hers; his breathing ragged, and stared into her eyes.

Prue reached for him, her eyes filled with love, and his mouth was on hers again.

After a long while, Nicholas eased himself out of her

embrace, stood up and lifted her into his arms. He carried her along the hall to his bedroom and laid her on his bed.

Their exquisite lovemaking continued for hours, and finally, when it was over, Nicholas looked deep into her eyes, brushed his fingertips gently across her cheek, waited a moment, then said, "I love you."

Prue was surprised by his admission. With everything that had happened between them, she never expected to hear him say those words so soon. She ran her fingers through his damp hair and kissed the top of his head. "I love you too." He was an amazing lover and she was content to be in his bed, in his arms, and realized he was hers after all.

Thirty seven

Prue woke up to an empty bed and wondered where Nicholas was. *Maybe he's in the shower.* She stretched her body and smiled as she recalled the way he had made love to her the previous evening. He knew exactly how to give her pleasure and she loved him for it. She sat up and glanced around the room, noticing her clothes sitting in the wing-backed armchair by the window.

She threw back the covers, stepped onto the polished wood floor and padded over to her clothes. She'd take a quick shower before heading to the kitchen, where she assumed Nicholas was, because he wasn't in the bathroom.

Dressed, and her hair towel dried, Prue felt refreshed and ready for breakfast. She opened the bedroom door and walked along the hallway, through the living room to the kitchen. Nicholas was at the counter making waffles, bacon and scrambled eggs. She smiled at the sight. He could cook. That was an endearing quality in a man.

Prue wandered over to him. "Good morning. That smells wonderful," she said, touching his arm and planting a kiss on his cheek.

"Morning." He continued to busy himself with the breakfast preparations and didn't look at her. "Why don't you take a seat. This is almost ready."

She frowned, walked over to the breakfast table and sat down. Two mugs of coffee were already waiting. She picked up hers and took a sip. Something didn't feel right.

Nicholas dished up the meals, brought them over to the table and joined her, setting a plate down in front of her. "Thank you. It looks amazing," she said, smiling up at him. He gave a thin smile and she knew he had something on his mind.

"You're welcome." He sat a napkin across his lap and picked up his knife and fork.

Prue watched him for a moment, her stomach doing a nervous flip. "Is something wrong, Nick?"

He set his cutlery down, stared into her eyes and waited a beat. "I think last night was a mistake. We got caught up in the moment, the wine…"

She couldn't believe what she was hearing. Prue was speechless.

"It shouldn't have happened. Nothing has been resolved between us. I don't know what we were thinking."

Tears stung Prue's eyes. How could he think their being together was a mistake?

His gaze moved to his plate and he picked up his cutlery then put it down again. "I'm sorry if I've hurt you that was the last thing I wanted to do."

Prue found her voice. "You're sorry? I can't believe you're saying this to me. You initiated last night. Kissed me, carried me to your bed. Made love to me… told me you loved me. For what? To tell me this morning it was a mistake?" A tear slid down her left cheek and she brushed it away.

"Look, I said I'm sorry. We'd had a bit to drink last night and…"

"Are you going to blame it on the alcohol?" She stood up. "Be a man, Nick. Take responsibility for what happened and don't make excuses."

He gazed up at her. "Prue, I'm…"

She raised a hand. "Don't say you're sorry. Just make

up your mind what you want." She headed to the door. "And don't follow me back to New York until you know." She marched out of the kitchen, through the living room to the entry hall, plucked her jacket off the rack and pushed her arms into it then threw her scarf around her neck and walked out the front door. Tears stung the backs of her eyes but she was determined not to give in to her emotions, not now.

Prue stalked down the steps toward her rental checking the pockets of her coat for the keys, realizing Nicholas had them. "Damn it." She huffed in frustration, turned around and headed back up the stairs to the porch. Nicholas was at the door holding up the car keys.

She snatched them from his hand without a word and descended the stairs again. She was so angry. How could she have been so stupid to think his making love to her had changed his mind? *Stupid, stupid, stupid.* Why hadn't she taken her own advice about not drinking too much and not making a fool of herself? She pressed the remote and climbed into the car.

What made the whole humiliating situation worse was that Nicholas didn't even bother to follow her.

Back at the inn, Prue pulled clothing from hangers and snatched garments from drawers as she hurried to pack. She had wanted to stay and sightsee, but now that was out of the question. Tears spilled down her face. Why had Nicholas been so cruel? Why had he slept with her only to tell her this morning it had been a mistake? A mistake? It wasn't as though he had written her name incorrectly in a book at one of his author signings. They had shared the most intimate moment together, shared their bodies, their souls. How could he dismiss it so easily?

A knock on the door caused her body to jump. She gasped and turned around, hoping it wasn't Nicholas. "Who is it?" She realized she shouldn't have answered.

"It's Peter Moncrieff, Nick's friend. Can I talk to you for a minute?"

Prue hesitated before walking across the room. *Why is he here?* She swung the latch back and opened the door. "Did Nick send you?"

He shook his head. "No, he doesn't know I'm here."

"Then why *are* you here?" She folded her arms.

He gave a wry smile. "I, uh, came to see if you're alright. Nick mentioned what happened."

She scowled and threw her hands up. "What? He told you about last night? How could he? That's so personal."

Peter raised his hands in defense. "Hey, I get that. I do. But he's pretty upset and I wanted to make sure…"

"He's upset? How do you think I feel?"

"I can only imagine."

"Right. You're his friend so you'd take his side."

"That's not how friendship works. If he's wrong I tell him he's wrong. And I don't agree with what he did, not at all." He motioned through the door. "May I come in?"

Prue shook her head. "I don't think so. You can go back and tell Nicholas Colton I'm not playing into his guilt game any longer. If he wants to work things out he can come and speak to me, when he figures out what he actually wants. If he ever does." She gave him a furtive glance. "Thanks for coming by. But I'm fine."

"Ok. If you're sure?" He admired her tenacity.

"Yes, I'm sure." She closed the door, folded her arms and huffed out an angry breath. How dare Nick confide their sexual misfortunes to his friend. Prue felt violated.

Thirty eight

Rachelle picked Prue up from the airport and the drive back to her friend's apartment was quiet for most of the way. Prue had called her but hadn't gone into detail over the phone as to why she had cut her trip short. Rachelle knew something had gone awry because Prue planned to be gone for several days. She glanced sideways at her friend wondering if she should ask the question.

Prue could sense Rachelle wanted to know what happened but she wasn't in the mood to talk about Nicholas Colton, nor his seduction and betrayal. She wanted to go home, hug her daughter and stay in the apartment for the rest of the leave she had left. Because her mind was somewhere else Prue knew she wouldn't be able to concentrate if she went back to work early.

Rachelle spotted a car leaving, indicated and pulled

into the curb. "Well, here we are safe and sound. I'm sure Nikki will be happy to see you." She smiled.

"Thanks for picking me up, Rache. I really appreciate it."

Rachelle's curiosity got the better of her. "Honey, what happened?" She gave Prue a concerned frown. "I can see how upset you are. Is there anything I can do?"

Prue shook her head. "Not at the moment but thanks for the offer. I'd rather not discuss what happened right now. I need to get my head around it first."

"Are you seeing Nick again?"

She shrugged. "Who knows? He changes his mind so often it's hard to keep up. I have no idea where I stand with him."

Rachelle rubbed Prue's arm. "I'm so sorry."

"Me too." She sighed and opened the car door. "Well thanks again for the lift. I'll grab my suitcase and you can head off." Prue pulled her bag out of the trunk, then went back to the open passenger window. "See you in a few days."

"Keep your chin up, hon. Things will work themselves out. You'll see."

Prue gave Rachelle a thin smile, waved goodbye and headed along the sidewalk to the front steps of her apartment building. It was good to be back on home territory.

Later that evening, after Nikki was tucked in bed, Prue sat on the sofa wrapped in her pink throw rug and sulked. Nicholas had treated her like nothing more than a one night stand, something he hadn't done all those years ago. She'd believed they had made a lasting intimate connection this time, so what went wrong? *'I think last night was a mistake'* popped into her head and a tear slid down her cheek. Why had he made their night together seem so cheap?

Her cell phone chimed and her body jolted back to the present. She had been lost in her thoughts. She snatched it off the coffee table and frowned at the screen. Prue didn't recognize the number. She answered, hoping it wasn't Nicholas. "Hello?"

"Hello. Is this Prue Granger?"

Prue's stomach flipped over. "Yes. Who's this?"

"I'm Nurse Mitchell at Allegheny General Hospital's Emergency Room…"

"Oh my God, what's happened? Are my parents ok?" The roads were slippery at this time of year and Prue hoped they hadn't been involved in a serious car accident.

"I'm calling about your brother, Toby. He's had a bit of a mishap. Fractured his pelvis and broke his left leg in a riding accident. He asked me to contact you. Are you able to come out here at all?"

"Are my parents with him?"

"No ma'am. They were here earlier but they've gone home for the evening."

It couldn't have come at worse time. Prue wasn't in the right frame of mind to be going home right now, still she had five days medical leave she could use and Toby was always there for her. "Please tell my brother we'll leave first thing in the morning and I'll see him some time tomorrow afternoon?"

"I'll do that ma'am. And don't worry. He's been given some heavy duty meds and is resting comfortably at the moment."

"Ok. Thank you so much for letting me know."

"You're welcome, ma'am. Have a good night."

"You too." Prue rang off. It was a risky business breaking in new horses, although Toby didn't do it as often anymore because he had trained riders to handle that side of the ranch, but that must have been how the accident happened. She glanced up at the wall clock. 9.00 p.m. She grabbed her laptop from her bedroom and sat down to check bus schedules. She booked two tickets on a Greyhound bus leaving at six o'clock the next morning. Lucky for her she hadn't unpacked hers or Nikki's suitcases yet.

Prue contacted Rachelle to let her know what had happened and told her she'd be away for the rest of the week, maybe longer. She'd have to cross that bridge when she came to it. She'd call once Toby was settled at home and something could be worked out to assist him while he was incapacitated. Rachelle asked Prue to give him her regards and hoped he made a speedy recovery.

Lying in bed in the early hours of the morning, Prue couldn't sleep once again. Her mind was full and her heart ached. She was worried about her brother, despite the nurse's assurance that he was fine, and she was worried about the whole Nicholas situation. Would they ever get the timing right? Did he even want to?

Prue glanced at the bedside clock radio. The green display read 3:02. If she didn't get at least an hour or two of rest she'd be a wreck by the time she arrived in Pittsburgh. And she didn't want to worry her brother or her parents. They had enough to deal with. She sighed and rolled onto her right side so she couldn't see the time. Prue tried counting sheep, but Nick's handsome face kept popping into her head. She gave another heavy sigh and flopped onto her back, staring up at the ceiling.

It would be good going back home again. She'd enjoyed spending the holidays with her family. While she had been there she hadn't given Nicholas Colton any thought, until she ran into him. Perhaps helping her brother out for a few days would take her mind off her problems. She could only hope.

Thirty nine

Nicholas was once again at his computer unable to put anything on the blank page in front of him. All he could think about was Prue and the way he'd acted toward her the morning after. Yes, they'd drank some wine, but neither of them had been intoxicated to the point that they didn't know what they were doing. And, yes, he had initiated them sleeping together. Why couldn't he get past the whole not knowing about his daughter before now situation and attempt to make a life with the woman he was in love with? Be a father to his child? What was wrong with him?

He gazed out the window at the darkening sky and sighed. He couldn't think about that now, he had to finish his next book by the fast-approaching deadline. But how was he supposed to do that when he couldn't get Prue out of his head? Nicholas knew he'd made another mistake where she was concerned. He'd walked away from her once and knew it had been the wrong decision. Now he was doing the same thing all over again.

The ringing doorbell pulled him from his thoughts. He gazed up from the computer screen and wondered who it was. He pushed himself out of his desk chair, strode through the living room and opened the door.

"Got a minute or are you in the middle of something?" Peter asked.

"No, come on in. I could use the distraction. Want some coffee?" He turned and headed to the kitchen.

"Yeah, thanks." Peter closed the front door and followed him through the living room. "I wanted to talk to you about Prue."

Nicholas took two mugs out of an overhead cupboard and sat them on the counter then glanced over his shoulder at his friend. "Oh? Why?"

Peter sighed, folded his arms and leaned against the doorframe. "I went to see her before she left."

Nicholas frowned. "You did? How come?"

"I wanted to make sure she was ok. It was pretty clear you weren't, and I thought someone should check on her."

"That was good of you. Thanks. I know it should've

been me but after what I said I didn't think she'd want to talk to me."

"No problem. She, uh, gave me a message for you."

He gave Peter a curious frown. "She did?"

"Yeah. She said she wasn't playing into your guilt games anymore and if you wanted to work things out to go talk to her when you made up your mind what you were doing. Oh, yeah, and she added if you ever do."

Nicholas swallowed hard. "Prue said that?"

"Yeah." Peter sat down at the breakfast table.

Nicholas brought over the coffee and joined him. "I know I treated her like a…well, I treated her badly. It's hard, you know? I want to get over the whole not knowing about Nikki thing, but something inside won't let me. Every time I come to the decision to let it go, a brick wall with Prue's name on it hits me in the face."

Peter leaned back in the chair and folded his arms. "Come on, Nick, that's a cop out and you know it. If you want to be with her you'll find a way to move forward. You have a beautiful woman out there who loves you and a lovely little girl. Go fight for them."

"I can't right now I have a deadline looming. The book has to be finished in four months. I can't keep dropping everything to fly across the country."

"Well you should."

Nicholas gave him a stern look. "Perhaps you're right, but I can't. I have to work."

Peter sighed. "And perhaps you're being stubborn. You need to let it go. If you don't you might not have a shot at all. It's up to you."

Forty

As the Greyhound bus pulled into the 11th Street transportation center, Prue spotted her mom's blue Ford Focus parked on the street. She packed away Nikki's coloring book and crayons, gathered up their belongings and prepared to get off the bus. It had been over a seven hour journey from New York to Pittsburgh and Prue needed some caffeine to perk her up before visiting her brother in the hospital.

Prue took her daughter's hand, grabbed the handle of her suitcase and made her way into the center to find her mother. Lorraine smiled and waved as the girls came through the automatic glass doors and Nikki tugged her hand free, let go of the handle of her small suitcase and ran over to her. "Hi, Grandma, we came on a big bus with a toilet in the back," she said, her little face beaming.

"Yes, honey, I know. Was it fun?" Lorraine picked up her granddaughter and gave her a big hug.

Nikki nodded with enthusiasm, a huge smile spreading across her face. "I colored in on the way. Do you wanna see my pictures?"

Lorraine stood Nikki on the floor then leaned in to give Prue a quick hug. "Maybe later, sweetie, when we get home. Right now we have to go visit your uncle at the hospital."

Nikki gave a sorrowful pout. "Poor uncle Toby. I hope the doctor makes him feel better."

The drive to Allegheny General would take around ten minutes with a quick stop to pick up coffee. Prue pulled her cosmetics bag out of her purse, opened the compact and sighed as she gazed at her grim reflection in the small round mirror. Lack of sleep had created dark circles under her eyes. She found her concealer and attempted to blend away the shadows. She didn't want Toby worrying about her state of health while he was recuperating.

Her mom glanced at her sideways. "Not getting enough sleep, honey?"

Prue sighed. "No, not lately."

"Anything you want to talk about?"

"I'll be fine. It usually sorts itself out after a while."
She touched her mother's arm. "Don't worry about me.
We've got bigger problems with Toby's recovery."

Lorraine frowned into the rearview mirror at her
daughter. "Don't change the subject, Prudence. What's
going on?"

Prue gave a frustrated huff. "Nothing's going on."

"You'd tell me if there was, wouldn't you?"

"Of course I would." She felt like a teenager again
being quizzed for some minor misdemeanor. "Seriously,
Mom, everything's fine." Prue finished applying her
makeup and lip gloss and pushed the small crimson bag
back into her purse. "There. That feels better."

Lorraine pulled into a parking spot outside Starbucks
on 6th Street. "What would you like?"

Prue dug into her purse looking for her wallet. "A
vanilla latte, thanks." She held up a ten dollar bill.

Her mom waved the money away and opened the car
door. "I got it. Back in a tick."

The drive from Starbucks to the hospital took all of
five minutes. Lorraine turned into James Street and drove
along the road to the hospital parking garage.

Prue gazed up at the oversized sign above the
entrance: ALLEGHENY GENERAL "ONE OF AMERICA'S

BEST HOSPITALS" —U.S. News & World Report. If that didn't elicit confidence in the abilities of the medical staff working at the hospital, nothing would. She was glad Toby was in good hands.

When Prue walked into Toby's room she found it difficult to hold back the tears threatening to spill. The sight of her brother lying in a hospital bed, his leg in a plaster cast, with scrapes and bruises on his face were too much for her already fragile emotions. She inhaled a breath to steady herself, rushed over to the bed and threw her arms around him. "Hey, big bro, what've you gone and done to yourself?"

He was groggy from the meds, but managed to wrap one arm around her and kiss the top of her head. His words were slurred. "Hi, little sis... I'm glad... you're here. It was a stupid accident. Came off of Demon hard, hit the dirt with my hip the wrong way and planted my face too."

Prue frowned. "I can see that. How are you feeling?"

"Like I've been run over by a train. But the meds are good. Takes the edge off." He attempted a smile.

So did Prue, although she was worried about him and knew it showed on her face. "How long are you here for?"

"They said I can go home in a week or two as long as

I get plenty of rest for the next eight to ten weeks and use a pair of crutches when I'm on my feet. The doc said the pelvis was a clean fracture, so was the leg. That's something, I guess."

"It sure is. Thank goodness you didn't need surgery." She sat in the visitor chair beside the bed. "I have a week off, so I'll do what I can to help you out while I'm here."

"I really appreciate it, sis. Nikki with you?"

She shrugged. "Where else would she be?"

"Can I see her?"

"Are you sure you're up to it. She's a bit boisterous right now. Long bus ride." She smiled.

"Yeah, I'm up to it. Don't care if she's full of beans. Bring her in."

Prue stood up. "Ok. Be right back."

"Thanks."

Nikki hurtled into the room. "Uncle Toby!" When she saw him lying in bed with his leg in a cast she stopped short, a frown of concern on her little face, then tiptoed over to him, her voice in a whisper. "Sorry, Uncle Toby, I'll be more quiet."

"Hey, Jellybean, how're ya doing? Enjoy the bus ride?" He patted the bed and Nikki climbed onto the chair, then onto the bed and wriggled up beside him.

"Yep. It was fun. There was a toilet on the bus? I had to go so mommy took me."

"Yeah? How was it?" His face lit up at the innocent conversation.

"It was small but it was okay. I used it while the bus was moving." She covered her mouth with her hand and giggled.

"Sounds neat." Toby tweaked his niece's nose.

Prue walked over to the bed. "Uncle Toby needs to rest now, honey. We'll come back and see him later. Ok?"

"Ok, Mommy." She leaned in, kissed her uncle on the forehead and tapped his cheek with the palm of her hand. "The doctor will make you all better soon, Uncle Toby. I love you."

Toby smiled. "I love you too, baby girl."

Prue kissed his forehead too. "We'll come back later. I need to go home to freshen up and give Nikki something to eat."

"That's ok. Do what ya gotta do. I'll still be here." He winked at her. "Love you, sis. Thanks for coming."

"Love you too. Where else could I be?" She repeated the words her brother had used when she'd told him about the lawyer Nicholas had hired. They would always be there for each other.

Lorraine crossed the room and kissed her son. "Rest up, honey. Dad's coming in later too."

"Thanks, Mom."

Out in the corridor, Prue glanced over her shoulder at Toby's hospital room door. She was glad he was ok and happy to be home to help him. Her family meant the world to her.

Later that evening, Toby asked Prue if she could hang back for a while, he had something he wanted to talk to her about. Prue arranged with her mom to drive the Focus back and Lorraine and Nikki went home with her dad. She was curious about what her brother wanted to say to her. He'd been turning something over in his mind the whole time they were visiting with him. She could see it on his face.

"I want to run something by you to see what you think. Ok?"

Prue nodded.

"I'm going to be off my feet for at least eight to ten weeks the doctor says, so I need someone I can rely on to run the ranch and do the admin stuff while I'm out of action." He took Prue's hand. "Would you consider staying on for a while? I can pay you a decent wage... it won't be as much as what you get now but it'll be enough to keep you and Nikki comfortable and do the necessities. I could really use your help."

Prue was surprised by Toby's offer. She loved her brother but she loved her job too and she had waited a long time to find exactly the right position for her. She didn't want to let Toby down, but how could she pick up and move back home when she'd created a life in New York for her and her daughter?

"Tobe, it's a generous offer..."

He nodded. "I understand. You love your job and where you live. You've made new friends too. It's ok, I'll work something out." The look of disappointment on his face made Prue's heart clench.

"Can I think about it?" She smiled and patted his hand.

Toby's face brightened. "Of course you can. I know it's a big ask. And I'll understand if you say you can't, but I'm hoping you might consider it."

"Let me think it over. Ok? I'll give you an answer by the end of the week, if not sooner."

"That's all I can ask for. Thank you." He squeezed her hand.

Forty one

When Prue arrived home her mother met her in the entry hall, before heading up to bed, to let her know she had kept dinner warm for her. Prue wasn't the least bit hungry but wouldn't tell her mom that because she had waited up for her.

She hung up her jacket, followed her mom into the kitchen and sat at the center island. It had been a long, exhausting day and she was tired. She gave a heavy sigh rested her elbows on the counter top and placed her chin in her hands.

Lorraine plated up Prue's dinner and set it down in front of her then took a seat on a nearby stool. She could see something was weighing on her daughter's mind. She didn't want to pry but did want to help relieve the burden her daughter appeared to be carrying. "Everything ok?"

Prue picked up her fork and played with her food. "Toby offered me a paid job working the ranch while he's recuperating."

Lorraine's eyebrows rose. "What did you tell him?"

"That I'd think about it." She sat her fork on the plate and threw her hands up. "What was I supposed to say? He's injured and needs my help."

Her mom rested a comforting hand on her arm. "Honey, if you'd prefer not to do it, tell him."

Prue sighed. "I don't want to let him down, especially not now. It wouldn't be fair."

"Are you ready to give up your life in New York? Your job? That wouldn't be fair either."

"I... don't know." She scooped food onto her fork but set it down again. "Toby's always there when I need him, willing to drop everything and come to my rescue."

Lorraine rubbed her daughter's arm. "I know, honey. But that's his choice. He's a grown man."

Prue frowned. "Yes, but..."

"Toby only wants you to be happy. If coming back home isn't the right thing for you, don't do it. He'll understand."

"I'm not sure if it is or not. I need some time to think it over."

Lorraine climbed off the stool and rested a hand on Prue's shoulder. "It's getting late, think about it tomorrow after a good night's sleep." She kissed her daughter's forehead. "Night, sweetie."

"Night, Mom. Love you."

"Love you too."

Once she was alone, Prue poured herself a mug of coffee and ate her dinner. New York was exciting and she'd made some wonderful friends there in the past year. So had Nikki. But family was the most important thing to her and she didn't want to disappoint her brother. He needed her help. Living in the country was always a great option for raising children: cleaner air, safe open spaces, and interactions with a variety of animals. It had worked before she and Nikki moved to The Big Apple so why wouldn't it again? Working at the ranch would be hard but fulfilling too. And who knew what the future held, she might buy into it and become her brother's business partner one day.

Prue grabbed a notepad and pen from off the desk in the study, took her seat at the counter and jotted down the pros and cons then calculated the funds she'd need to make the move. The apartment came furnished, so it was just a matter of boxing up hers and Nikki's personal effects and having them freighted home. She knew her daughter would be overjoyed to have grandma, grandpa and uncle Toby around more often and it had always been a good environment for her. Was she considering it? Prue needed to be sure before she made a final decision.

A couple of days later, Prue borrowed her mother's car and took a drive. Her heart thudded as she drove up the dirt drive, under the canopy of yellowwoods, to the building site. It had been eight years since she'd been to her unfinished home and she wasn't sure she was up to setting foot on the acres of land that held her empty dreams.

She maneuvered the bright blue Ford Focus to the right side of the open gates, turned off the engine and breathed a heavy sigh. Connor loved this particular piece of the country and had wanted to build their perfect home for the family they'd planned to have.

Prue remained in the car contemplating whether or not she would actually step out and walk over to the two-story house. The unfinished remnants of a life that wasn't meant to be. A tear slid down her cheek and a painful lump formed in her throat as she sniffed back the urge to cry. The grief inside her had never truly disappeared. How could it when Connor had been the only man she had ever loved? And she still missed him.

The realtor would arrive at any minute and Prue needed to pull herself together. Today would be the hardest day of her life (apart from losing Connor) but she had to do it. She had to let go of the past so she could move forward, hopefully into a future with Nicholas.

A white Hyundai Elantra pulled in beside the Focus and a well-groomed woman dressed in a cherry red jacket and black pants stepped out of it.

Prue brushed the tear from her cheek, sniffled, took a quick glance in the rearview mirror to check her mascara hadn't run and climbed out of the car.

The thirty-something brunette walked over to her and extended her hand. "Hello there, you must be Prue. I'm Miranda. We spoke on the phone." The women shook hands and the realtor gazed around the tree-lined acres then studied the semi-completed home. "It's a beautiful spot out here. So, you're considering selling the block with the unfinished house on it?"

Prue glanced over her shoulder at the vacant structure sitting center stage, still uncertain if she'd made the right decision, then her eyes returned to the woman in front of her. She sighed. "Uh… yes, I think I am."

"Alright. Why don't you show me around so I can get an idea of what the property is worth and we can go from there? Did you have a price in mind?"

"No, not really. I was hoping you could tell me that." Prue hesitated for a moment before heading to the semi-finished porch. "Please, come this way." The women climbed the front steps and Prue took a key from the pocket of her jeans and opened the door. She swung it back and motioned for the realtor to go in ahead of her.

Miranda stepped across the threshold into the entry hall, stopped and turned around. Prue was still on the porch, the color had drained from her face. The realtor knew the tragic story of the young engaged couple (it had been big news back then) and didn't want to pressure Prue into doing something she wasn't ready to do. "Why don't I take a look around while you wait out here? I won't be too long. Mind if I take a couple pictures on my phone?"

Prue breathed a relieved sigh. "No, not at all. Thank you for understanding."

Miranda nodded then disappeared into what would be the living room, once finished, and continued on through the lower and upper levels of the house.

After ten minutes she came out onto the porch. "I think it has great selling potential. The kitchen and bathrooms are completed which is a plus and it would make a comfortable single family home. Being unfinished it also offers the buyer an opportunity to make the place their own." She turned around and gazed back through the open door then looked at Prue. "Let me speak to my property manager and see what I can do. I'd like to get the best possible price for you." She smiled.

"I'd appreciate that, Miranda. Thank you so much."

"My pleasure. I'll give you a call as soon as I've spoken with her and we can work out the details."

"Ok. I'll wait for your call. Thank you for coming all the way out here." Prue locked the front door.

The women walked back to their cars together.

"By the way, how's your brother doing? I heard he came off one of his horses and is in Allegheny General."

"He broke his pelvis and left leg in the accident, but he's doing ok. The doctor said he might be able to come home sooner than expected."

"That's good news. I'm so pleased he's ok. He's a nice man."

"You know him?"

"Yes. My daughter takes riding lessons out at Black Stallion."

"Oh. That's great."

They stopped by Prue's car.

"Thanks for contacting us and considering Northwood Realty to list your home. I think someone will snap it up once it's on the market. The house has a number of appealing features people will be looking for in a family home, especially that gorgeous fireplace in the living room." She held out her hand and Prue shook it. "Take care, Miss Granger. I'll be in touch."

"You too. Thank you." Prue watched the realtor leave then turned around and ran her eyes over the house once more before getting into her mom's Ford and driving away. She hoped selling it was the right thing to do.

Forty two

Nicholas had his revised and edited manuscript completed within two months and had sent a hardcopy to his publisher first thing that morning. He had finished it in record speed because he wanted to take some time away from writing and fly to New York to talk to Prue. The book had been all-consuming, but now that it was done he was prepared to make every effort to work things out with her. He'd been a fool to let her walk out of his life again and he could only blame himself if she was no longer willing to talk to him.

He organized a New York flight for the same afternoon. He wasn't about to waste any more time debating over whether or not he should go. He was going. The following morning he'd head straight to the broadcast center and beg Prue to give him another chance. Pete had been right. He should have abandoned the book and flown to The Big Apple when things first fell apart. Two months? Would she even want to see him now? All he could do was hope.

After arranging his flight, accommodation and taxi, Nicholas closed his MacBook and headed to his bedroom. He'd have a suitcase packed and ready to go in less than half an hour. It was time to begin a new phase in his life with the woman he loved and his little girl. He still couldn't get his mind around the fact that he was a dad, but he loved the idea. He hoped Nikki would like him when she met him, at least until she got to know him, then he hoped she would love him because he already loved her.

Nicholas wheeled his navy blue American Tourister suitcase along the hallway, stood it by the front door and checked that the dogs had enough food and water until Pete came by to pick them up. They were staying with him this time.

The taxi pulled into the drive and the driver beeped the horn. Nicholas' American Airlines flight departed at 12.20 p.m. so he needed to get a move on. He opened the front door, grabbed the handle of his case and stepped out onto the porch. His stomach shrank into a tight knot as he closed the door and headed down the steps. What kind of reception would Prue give him when he arrived at her place of work?

Gazing out of the airplane window, Nicholas thought about what he'd say when he saw Prue again. The first thing he would do was apologize for the way he had treated her the morning after their exquisite night together, which he knew had been anything but a mistake. He adored making love to her. The intimacy of his skin on hers awakened his soul and made his body come alive. He recalled how willing Prue had been to give herself to him and how much he'd wanted her. How his hands had roamed every inch of her and the way her body had responded to his touch. Their lovemaking had surpassed everything they'd shared that night all those years ago. Nicholas knew they were meant to be together and he wasn't about to do anything else to ruin that chance.

The stopover in Phoenix had been delayed, so the flight wouldn't arrive at JFK Airport until the early hours of the morning. When he arrived at his hotel he'd head straight to his suite and try to get some sleep so that he was clear-headed for the following day. He wanted to pour his heart out to Prue without any mishaps this time. Tell her how much she meant to him and how much he wanted to be a father to their daughter. He wanted them to be a family.

An image of Prue popped into Nicholas' thoughts and he smiled. He hoped he would get to wake up next to that lovely face every morning for the rest of his life.

Forty three

Prue knew making the decision to move back home had been the right one. Nikki was happy, she was happy, and all thoughts of Nicholas Colton were no longer the center of her existence, although he still hovered in the back of her mind and she wondered if she'd ever see him again. Rachelle had been upset but understood why Prue had to leave. Family came first. Always. She'd promised they would remain *friends for life*, but Prue knew that would change over time and eventually they would stop speaking. A sad reality.

Although Toby's broken leg had healed, his pelvis was still mending. The doctor told him it may take another month before he was completely healed, and that there were no guarantees he wouldn't experience some painful side effects from time to time for the rest of his life.

Prue helped him out onto the front porch of his home at the ranch and made him comfortable on the outdoor lounge under the window. She knew how much her brother hated being unable to work and ride but did her best to reassure him that once his body mended he'd be back doing what he loved. He was an independent man who handled his own life and it was difficult for him not to be managing ranch business.

She rearranged the cushions behind him. "There. Comfortable?"

Toby looked up at her. "Yep. Thanks, sis."

"Can I get you anything before I head to the office?"

"Nope. I think I've got everything I need." He had on his Stetson, his cell phone was in his hand, and a mystery novel and a glass of juice sat on the small, round table beside him. "Besides, I'm not an invalid I can still do some things for myself. You're not here to be at my beck and call, you're here to run things while I can't."

"I know. But, you're meant to be taking it easy. If you need anything just text me, I'm only a few hundred feet away." She gazed across the grass at the detached wooden structure next to the stables. "We'll take a slow walk around the property later so you can get your exercise. Ok?"

"Sure. How's it all going by the way? You haven't said much since you moved back."

"I think I've got everything under control. The riders and trainers seem to have warmed to me now. That's something. And the stable hands have never had a problem with me from day one." She gave him a thin smile.

"They'd better treat you with respect or they'll have me to deal with." Toby folded his arms.

"Hey, it's all good. Trust me. I won't take anyone's rubbish."

"I'm glad you've settled in, but the ranch wasn't exactly what I meant."

"Oh. Everything else is fine. Nikki's happy to be spending time with her gran and poppie and I'm doing something I enjoy." She gazed at the trees in the distance. "I love this place."

"What about...?"

She gazed at her brother and raised her hand. "Let's not spoil a perfect morning, ok?" As she turned to walk down the front steps a car drove through the ranch gates. "I wonder who that could be."

Toby pushed himself up off the cushions and scrutinized the vehicle as it moved closer. "Don't recognize the car. Maybe it's a new client."

"Mm, maybe." Prue descended the steps and waited for the silver sedan to pull into a parking spot in front of the office. When the door opened and Nicholas got out she almost swallowed her tongue. "Oh, my God!"

Toby eased himself into a sitting position. "You want me to talk to him?"

Prue glanced over her shoulder and motioned for him to stay put. "No, it's ok. I'll do it." She walked over to Nicholas standing beside the car. "What are you doing here?"

"I flew to New York two days ago and went to the broadcast center. They told me you'd left, so I…"

"Did Rachelle tell you where I was?" She folded her arms.

"After some heckling, yes. She didn't want to though so don't be mad at her." He closed the car door. "Can we talk? Please?"

Prue gave her brother a sideward glance. "Now's not a good time. I have lots to do."

Nicholas touched her arm. "When would be a good time? I'm not here to make your life difficult I just want to talk to you."

Prue's eyes returned to him. "Maybe you should've thought of that before you told me our night together was a mistake. You didn't even come after me to apologize. It's been two months and I haven't heard a word from you."

"I know and it was wrong of me, I should have. I'm sorry." His eyes reflected the anguish inside him for causing her more pain.

Her serious expression softened. "Why didn't you? Do you really believe that night was a mistake?"

"No." He shook his head. "No I don't believe it was a mistake. I don't know why I said it. I guess I was worried things were moving in a direction I wasn't prepared for." He sighed. "That's not what I mean."

"What *do* you mean?" She frowned. "Why *are* you here, Nick?"

"I'm here because I want to be a part of yours and Nikki's life. I know my actions haven't proved that but it's the truth. Before I knew about our daughter I was trying to find you so I could tell you that I wanted you in my life. There hasn't been anyone since that night. There couldn't have been because I fell in love you back then."

Prue glanced across the lawn at Toby and he nodded.

"Alright. Let's go for a drive and talk."

Nicholas' eyebrows rose. "Now?"

"Isn't that why you came here?"

"Yes. There's nothing I want more."

♥

Nicholas pulled the rental off the road under a huge tree and turned off the engine. The half hour drive had been in silence and he wondered what was going through Prue's mind. He needed to know. She sat in the passenger seat with her arms folded, gazing out of the window. He turned to her, a serious expression on his face, and reached across to touch her arm. "Prue?"

She turned her head. "Yes?"

"What can I do to make things right? How can I prove myself?" He gave her a pained frown.

Prue shrugged. "I'm not sure you can. Every time we come together to talk things through something goes wrong and we end up not talking at all. I can't be afraid to tell you how I feel and worry about how you'll react."

Nicholas sighed. "I know. But what you told me at the café threw me off balance. I couldn't get my head around it and I couldn't think straight. I never meant to hurt you. And that night at my house… it couldn't have been more perfect. I've been a stubborn fool. I hope you can find it in your heart to forgive me."

"When you told me our lovemaking had been a mistake I was devastated. I didn't understand how you could make love to me and then dismiss it so easily."

"I don't know what came over me that morning. All I could think about was the way we'd made love to each other, but then I ruined it by opening my mouth and saying something that deep down I didn't mean." He rubbed her arm. "I'm in love with you, Prue. I have been since the first time I laid eyes on you."

Tears stung the backs of Prue's eyes and she blinked back the urge to cry. "I'm in love with you too, Nick. I have been since that night all those years ago. But…"

He took her hands in his. "Then let's not waste any more time. Let's make a fresh start right here, right now."

Prue gave him an uncertain frown. "How can we after everything that's happened?"

"I am so sorry for every thoughtless thing I've done to sabotage us being together. I let pride stand in the way of what I really wanted and I should've known better. I love you and if you'll have me I'd like to be your husband one day."

Prue's eyes widened. "Are you… are you proposing?"

"In a manner of speaking, yes. I'd prefer to ask you over dinner some time soon with the perfect accessory to place on your finger." He took her hand. "What do you say? Want to make our family of three official?"

She stared deep into his eyes. "Are you sure, Nick? I wouldn't want to give you an answer and have you change your mind."

"I couldn't be more sure." Nicholas kissed the palm of her hand. "Is that a yes?"

Forty four

Toby had called his mom to ask her to bring Nikki over to the ranch. He thought when Prue and Nicholas returned their daughter should be there to greet them. He suspected the couple would work out their differences, which was long overdue, and by the time they came back their relationship would be in a much better place. At least he hoped it would.

He and Nikki were in the living room watching a Sesame Street DVD when he heard a car pull in. Toby eased himself up off the sofa and made his way out to the front porch. Prue and Nicholas were walking hand in hand across the grass, smiling and talking. It made Toby's heart happy.

"Hey, you two, nice to see ya smiling." He leaned on the railing.

"Thanks, big brother. It's good to be smiling."

Nikki raced out of the front door. "Mommy!" she squealed, launching herself at her mother.

Prue dropped Nicholas' hand and swung her daughter into the air then hugged her tight. "Hey, baby girl, did grandma bring you?"

Her little girl nodded. "Uncle Toby called and asked if she could."

Prue narrowed her eyes at her brother. "He did, did he?" She stood her daughter on the bottom front step.

Nikki looked up at Nicholas. "Hello. Who are you?"

Toby turned around and headed back into the house. It was time to give them some space.

Nicholas squatted in front of Nikki and was about to speak when Prue placed a hand on his shoulder.

"Honey, remember asking me about your daddy?"

Her daughter nodded, a look of uncertainty crossing her little face.

"Well, this is…"

Nikki's face lit up. "The man in the picture on the back of the scary book you were reading."

Nicholas glanced up at Prue and her cheeks flushed. "Uh, yes, that's right, but…"

Her little girl's eyes widened along with her mouth

and she looked at Nicholas and then her mom. "Is he my daddy?"

Prue nodded. Tears welled in her eyes and she couldn't speak.

Nikki launched herself into Nicholas' arms and held him tight. "I'm glad you came home, Daddy. I love you."

Nicholas wrapped his arms around her and stood up, looking over at Prue with tears in his eyes. "I love you too, sweetheart." He held his little girl just as tight, never expecting to hear those words so soon, and felt his heart would burst with joy.

Prue wrapped her arms around them both. It was a perfect moment.

Later that evening, Prue and Nicholas were sitting out on the front porch of the ranch house. It had been the most amazing day and neither of them wanted it to end. Prue was so happy that their daughter had accepted Nicholas as her daddy and she was excited about the prospect of them sharing a wonderful life together.

Nicholas kissed her forehead. "It's been an incredible day, better than I could ever have hoped for. I love you and I love our little girl."

Prue gave a happy sigh. "Yes, it has been. I love you

too, Nick, with all my heart and I'm so happy Nikki feels the same way about you. You two get on so well it's as though you've always been in her life. How is that possible?"

He slid an arm around her shoulders. "I don't know, but I'm glad it is. She's so adorable."

"Yes, she is." Prue rested her head on Nicholas' shoulder. "I never expected you to love her right away. I thought it would take time for the both of you."

"How could I not love her, Prue? She's ours." He pulled her closer. "She looks like me when I was that age, you know."

Prue sat up and looked at him. "She does?"

He nodded.

"It was such a surprise finding out your name. My calling her Nicole was so strange. It was as though you and I had a psychic connection or something."

He smiled. "Who knows? Maybe we do. Nicole Grace Colton has a nice ring to it, don't you think?"

She snuggled into him, sliding her arm around his middle. "Yes, it does. So does Prue Lorraine Colton."

Nicholas eased her away from him with a look of surprise. "Are you saying yes?"

Prue nodded, a broad smile spreading across her face.

"I'm the happiest man alive right now." He leaned in and kissed her long and slow.

Forty five

Three months later

Nicholas had been holding on to a secret for quite some time and didn't know how to raise the subject with Prue. It was something he had strong feelings about at the time, but now he wasn't sure if he'd made the right decision. How could he tell his beautiful fiancée what he had done? Would she understand his reasons when he explained them to her?

Their wedding was only two weeks away (Prue wanted a June date) and he needed to get the burden off his shoulders before they tied the knot. She would find out soon enough, even if he didn't tell her, and what then? He knew he couldn't keep it from her any longer.

Nicholas paced his empty office. He had already freighted his belongings and dogs to his new home—their new home—and was in the process of finalizing the sale of his Monterey cliffside cabin to a big screen, well-known action hero who wanted it as a vacation spot.

It had been Nicholas' retreat after Pam passed away. He couldn't have remained in the house they had lived in, where she had succumbed to the deadly disease, a place that reminded him of her suffering rather than the love they had shared there. He'd sold it as soon as he could and bought the house overlooking the ocean, a place he'd loved living and writing in for the past eight years. He would miss his best pal, Pete, but knew they would remain friends even with the distance between them.

He had no regrets. He was about to begin a new phase in his life with the woman he loved and his little girl. What more could he ask for? After taking one last look around, Nicholas closed the front door and handed the keys to the realtor for the new owner, then descended the steps and climbed into the taxi. In a few hours he would be at home with his mom and dad preparing for his wedding day. He couldn't wait to be Prue's husband.

His parents adored Prue and Nikki and were overjoyed to be grandparents again. They had taken to his daughter as though she had always been a part of their lives and he loved them for it. When he'd told them about the night he and Prue first met and the events leading up to them finding each other again, his parents were so happy he'd found the woman he wanted to spend the rest of his life with. He knew without a doubt that she was the one for him.

The taxi arrived at Monterey airport twenty minutes later. Nicholas paid the driver, grabbed his travel bag and headed for the main terminal. Once inside, he called Prue to let her know he was on his way. "Hello, darling, I'm at the airport now. I should arrive in a few hours. I've emailed you the flight details so you'll know what time to pick me up. I can't wait to see you, either. Give our girl a kiss from me. Love you too." He smiled as he pushed his phone into the pocket of his jeans and headed to the departure lounge. It was a good feeling having someone to come home to.

It was strange not writing on the flight and Nicholas felt at a loss as to what to do. Whenever he flew he worked on his next book and always managed to get a lot done during those long hours in the air. He supposed he could pull his iPad out of his bag and watch a movie or read a book, but neither option appealed to him.

His publisher had emailed a couple days before to say his next book would be released in a few weeks (after his wedding and honeymoon, of course) and wanted to know if he'd be available for book signings. He emailed back saying he wanted to take a short break while he spent time with his new family and told her he'd be in touch in a month or two.

Nicholas' mind wandered back to the secret he was about to reveal to Prue and his stomach tightened. How would she react to his confession?

Prue couldn't wait to pick Nicholas up from the airport. It had been a few weeks since she'd seen him because he'd flown home to organize the move and the sale of his house. His belief was he could write anywhere and he had no intention of disrupting Nikki's life by moving her and Prue to Monterey. While he was away, Prue made wedding preparations. She had contacted Rachelle and asked her to be a bridesmaid, to which her friend had answered with an excited yes! Prue also asked her closest friends in Pittsburgh, Laura, her high school friend, and two colleagues, Cathy and Bernadette, from her previous job at the local television station.

Her wedding dress had arrived and was hanging in a clear plastic cover on the closet door in her room. It was exquisite. She had chosen a beaded, white lace and charmeuse satin, backless, floor-length slip dress with scalloped lace V-neckline and elegant appliquéd train. Nikki's chiffon and tulle lilac flower girl dress had arrived at the same time, and the bridesmaid dresses would be delivered the next week, so, at least, that was one important component taken care of.

Prue's mom offered to make the wedding cake. Not only was she an amazing cook but also an incredible baker and Prue knew the cake would be divine. They'd chosen a buttercream, three tier basket design with crystallized flowers – lilac pansies, lemon roses, violets, cornflowers and lavender circling each row. And her mom would also make miniature copies of one tier for guests to take home.

Nicholas and his wedding party would wear charcoal gray suits with white shirts, lilac long ties and corresponding pocket handkerchief to match the bridesmaid outfits. He had asked his friend, Peter Moncrieff, to be his best man and Lloyd, Toby, and another friend, Jake, to be his groomsmen.

The author had made a reservation with the LeMont Restaurant for their wedding reception and a pre-wedding dinner. He was of the opinion that the elegant ambiance of the venue was the perfect complement to a wonderful ceremony and to his beautiful bride.

Everything was coming together and Prue couldn't have been happier, nor could she wait to become Mrs. Prue Colton.

ॐ ♥ ॐ

Prue waited at the arrivals lounge for Nicholas to disembark. Her heart did a little skip when he came through the door and she rushed over to greet him. Before she could say anything, Nicholas moved her to one side and pressed his mouth to hers in a long, slow hello kiss. Prue's head was dizzy with delight. They had missed each other so much.

When their lips parted Prue gave a happy sigh. "Wow!" Her face was aglow and her smile widened.

"It's so good to be back here with you. I've missed you both." He wrapped an arm around her shoulder as they headed out of the airport.

"We've missed you too. I've been busy though. The wedding plans are coming together beautifully. Everything's almost done."

"That's great news. It's going to be a wonderful day." He smiled and kissed her forehead.

"Yes, it is."

Nicholas was glad Prue hadn't brought Nikki along to pick him up. He wanted to talk to her about his secret and thought while they were alone was as good a time as any. On the drive out to his parents' home, he asked Prue to pull off the road for a moment.

Once the car was stopped he turned to her. "Darling, there's something I need to tell you before our wedding day."

Prue frowned. "Sounds serious." She reached over and took his hand.

He sighed. "It could be."

"I don't understand."

"You remember me saying I had a surprise for you?"

She smiled. "Yes, of course I do. A special wedding gift."

Nicholas placed his other hand on hers. "It is, yes." He sighed again. "It's difficult to explain though. Perhaps it would be better if I show you."

"Now? Isn't it meant to be a surprise for our wedding day?"

"I think you need to see it before then. Let me drive."

They changed seats and Nicholas pulled the car back onto the road.

There would still be enough daylight when they

arrived for him to show her what he'd kept from her for so long. Nicholas' heart thudded as he drove toward their destination. What would Prue say when she figured out where he was taking her?

When he turned onto the dirt drive her gaze fixed on him and she folded her arms. "Why are we here?" Her voice was defensive.

He continued under the canopy of trees. "You'll see in a minute."

Nicholas pulled the car up out front of the two-story, immaculate house, got out of the car and walked around to open Prue's door. He held out his hand to her. "Coming?"

Prue shook her head. "Who lives here now?"

"We do. At least we will after our wedding."

Her eyes widened. "No!" She continued shaking her head in disbelief.

"Darling, please come take a look."

"I can't believe you bought it." Prue scowled at him. "When the realtor told me the buyer wanted to remain anonymous I didn't understand why. Now I do. How did you know about the house?"

"I was looking for a home to renovate and saw it online. I didn't know it was yours until I spoke to Miranda and she told me the story behind the sale. That's when I knew I had to buy it. Will you please let me explain and if you're still unhappy with my reasons we'll sell the house. Ok?"

She sighed. "I don't want to live here, Nick. Why did you do this?"

He squatted by the open car door and took her hands in his. "We've both suffered terrible losses. Something neither of us will ever truly get over. I understand how you felt when you lost Connor because I felt exactly the same way losing Pam. I thought my world had ended, and without her in my life I wanted it to. Even though we've had the good fortune of falling in love with each other our lost loves will always live in our hearts. Where else could they be? Connor was the love of your life; you'd been together since you were kids. I couldn't ask you to forget him any more than you could ask me to forget Pam. I wanted this home to be his legacy to you, something tangible to remember him by."

Prue's eyes stung and a painful lump formed in her throat. She gave a heavy sigh and her tear-filled eyes moved to the front of the house. It was beautiful. Nicholas had created a stunning home for them to share. She spoke in a quiet voice. "I appreciate your heartfelt sentiment, Nick, I do. But I don't think I have the strength to live here. The memories are too painful. I want us to be happy, not have a cloud of sorrow hanging over our life together."

Nicholas followed her gaze. "I don't believe there would be. I think this home would become what Connor wanted for you. A place filled with love and happiness." He turned to her. "Are you sure you don't want to see inside?"

She shook her head.

He sighed. "Ok. We'll head back then."

The drive to Nicholas' parents' home was silent and he could see Prue was in quiet contemplation. Was she hurt? Was she angry? Was she reconsidering their wedding plans? He reached for her hand. "Talk to me, darling. Let's not hold things inside and not discuss them with each other. I'll do whatever you ask. I'll put the house on the market and sell it, if that's what you want."

Prue glanced at him. "I have nothing to say."

"Are you sure? You seem to be doing a lot of thinking over there." He gave a thin smile.

"I'm sure." She turned and gazed out of the passenger window again.

*F*orty six

Nicholas and Prue's wedding day had finally arrived and the beautiful spring morning—radiant sunshine, blue sky dotted with fluffy white clouds and a warm gentle breeze—held the promise of a wonderful open-air ceremony. It couldn't be more perfect.

Family and friends living in other states drove or flew in a couple of days before, and on the eve of the couple's nuptials, everyone attended a pre-wedding dinner at LeMont restaurant. It had been a night of excellent food, great wine and good conversation which had continued on into the early hours of the morning. Marriage officiant, Audrey Williams, had been the first to leave the venue at midnight saying she'd see the couple outside the Allegheny Observatory the next afternoon at 3.30 p.m.

Prue hadn't mentioned the house since the night

Nicholas had taken her to see it, and he wondered if she'd made a decision. He hadn't wanted to spoil the excitement of their approaching wedding day by bringing it up and decided to wait for the right time after their honeymoon.

The author had arranged a romantic tropical getaway with reservations at a five star Tahitian resort. The couple's opulent bungalow accommodation sat above the crystal clear water of a white sandy beach and he couldn't wait to arrive at their blissful destination and have his new bride all to himself for a while.

Nikki would be staying with both sets of grandparents during the four weeks her parents were away and she was excited to have a new gran and poppie to spend time with.

Prue, Nikki and her bridesmaids were preparing for the big day. The hair and makeup artist had arrived at 9.30 and started working on the women at ten o'clock. Prue, being the bride, was the last one to be styled so that her makeup looked fresher for longer.

Rachelle had flown in the day before and was staying with Prue at her parents' house. It had been great catching up and spending time together, and Prue realized how much she had missed her friend.

Nicholas and the men of his bridal party were at his parents' home. Pete had arrived early that morning, unable to get away any sooner as he'd been working on a case. Nicholas was finding it difficult to get used to his friend's new look. The PI had his wavy, collar-length sandy locks trimmed and was clean-shaven, a far cry from the rugged guy who usually appeared on the author's doorstep.

The bridal cars would arrive at three to take Nicholas and his entourage to Riverview Park. The couple had chosen classic Ford Model A silver and black hard tops as their mode of wedding transportation. And having the domed and columned observatory building as the backdrop for the ceremony would lend a feeling of elegance to their perfect day.

Although he couldn't wait to be married to Prue, Nicholas' stomach did uneasy flip flops and his palms were sweaty. He inhaled a deep breath and blew it out as he shrugged into his charcoal gray suit coat.

Peter could see his friend was nervous and brought him a glass of scotch. "Here, this'll do the trick. It'll take the edge off." He handed the drink to his friend and slapped him on the back. "Bottoms up."

Nicholas downed the alcohol in one swallow and coughed as it slid into his irritable stomach. He passed the glass back to his friend. "Thanks. Have you got the rings?" His voice sounded anxious even to him.

Peter dug into the inner pocket of his coat and pulled out the two, small velvet bags. "Don't worry. All taken care of." He pushed them back into place. "Relax."

❧ ♥ ❧

The first car arrived at Prue's parents' house right on three. Her mom, Nikki and the bridesmaids went ahead to wait for her to arrive. Her dad was in the kitchen talking to the caterer who had come by to collect the wedding cake and Prue was putting some finishing touches to her outfit: something old, something new, something borrowed, something blue. She wore a pair of crystal stud earrings that had belonged to her grandmother, a diamond bracelet borrowed from Rachelle, her garter was blue and of course her wedding attire was new. The second Ford Model A would arrive in half an hour to take her and her father to the park, so she could be traditionally late to her wedding.

When three thirty came around and the car arrived Prue's dad called up the stairs. "Sweetheart, the car's here. Ready to walk down the aisle with your old dad?" He couldn't wait to see his beautiful girl in her wedding dress.

Prue didn't answer.

Martin frowned, climbed the first few steps and tried again. "Prue, the car's here."

Still no answer.

He climbed the stairs, walked along the hall to Prue's room and knocked. "Everything alright in there?" He opened the door to find the bedroom empty. Martin continued down the hall to the bathroom. "Honey, are you in there?" It was empty too. "Where could she be?"

Had Prue left with the women and didn't tell him? He called his wife's cell. "Lori, is Prue with you?"

"What do you mean 'is Prue with me'? Isn't she with you?" She ran her eyes around the guests and Nicholas and his group standing with the marriage officiant.

Martin was flustered. "Well, no, I can't find her."

"Have you checked everywhere?"

"Of course I have. She's not here."

"Where could she be? What am I supposed to tell Nick?"

"Don't tell him anything yet. I'll be there in a while and we can talk to him together."

"Marty, I'm worried about her. Do you think she'll show up?"

"I don't know. I don't understand why she's gone. Did she say anything to you?"

"No, not a thing. I thought everything was fine."

"The car's out front. I'll be there soon."

"Ok, hon. See you when you get here." Lorraine sighed as she slipped her phone into her purse. *Where are you, Prue?*

*F*orty seven

Lorraine was standing on the lawn beside the road when the bridal car pulled up opposite the observatory. She stepped up and opened the door for her husband and he climbed out. "Any word?" he asked, hoping their daughter had called her mother.

She shook her head. "No. Nothing." She turned to look at Nicholas and his groomsmen standing across the lawn. "What are we going to tell Nick?"

"The only thing we can tell him. The truth." He followed her gaze to their future son-in-law and sighed. "Let's get it over with." He took his wife's hand and they headed over to the author.

Nicholas beamed as they came toward him and Lorraine's heart clenched. How would he take the news?

"Nick, can we talk to you for a minute over there?"

Martin pointed to a nearby tree and he and Lorraine made their way over to it.

"Of course." He followed the pair into the shade.

"I, uh, don't know how to tell you this…"

Nicholas rested his hands on his soon-to-be father-in-law's shoulders. "What is it?"

Martin cleared his throat. "We, uh, we can't find Prue."

The smile disappeared from Nicholas' face and his hands dropped from the older man's shoulders. "What?" A look of confusion crossed his face. "What do you mean you can't find her?"

"When I called upstairs to tell her the car had arrived… she, she wasn't there."

An anxious frown replaced the confusion. "Did she say anything beforehand?"

"No," Lorraine said. "As I told Marty, she hadn't mentioned that anything was wrong."

Nicholas paced once, stopped and looked at Lorraine. "Prue didn't mention the wedding gift I bought for her, did she?"

She shook her head. "No. Why would she?"

He sighed. "Because I bought the house Connor was building and had it finished."

Lorraine's mouth gaped and her eyes widened. "You did? Why?"

"I know how much he meant to her. I thought it would be a nice legacy."

"Oh, Nick." She gave him a pained frown, her hand on her heart. "That's it… that must be why she ran off."

Nicholas' eyes lit up. "I think I know where she is. May I borrow your car?"

Lorraine handed him her keys. "Drive safely."

"I will. Please tell Audrey there's been a slight delay."

"Of course." She waved him off. "Go find your bride."

Nicholas headed for the bridal car he had arrived in.

❧ ♥ ☙

When Nicholas arrived at Prue's parents' home he headed straight to the garage. Her mom's blue Ford was there but her father's four wheel drive was missing. He climbed into the hatchback, reversed out of the garage and sped off.

Why hadn't she talked to him about her feelings? Why had she waited until their wedding day to do something about it? He pulled his cell phone from the inner pocket of his suit coat and pressed Prue's number.

The phone went to voicemail. He stuffed the phone back into his pocket and accelerated. He had to find her.

Half an hour later, he turned onto the dirt drive and drove to the double gates. Pulling the car up at the front steps, Nicholas threw the door open, climbed out and raced onto the porch. The front door was open. He stepped across the threshold, the one he should have carried Prue over, and rushed into the living room. She wasn't there. "Prue? Prue, where are you?"

She appeared at the top of the stairs. She was a vision in her wedding gown. "I'm here," she said in a quiet voice.

Nicholas could see she'd been crying. He climbed the steps to her. "Darling, why did you run off like that? Your mom and dad were worried about you. So was I."

Prue gazed up at him, tears slipping down her face. "I – I needed time to think."

"About us?"

She shook her head. "I had a dream about Connor last night. He told me to be happy." She sniffled and more tears spilled.

Nicholas pulled her into his arms and held her tight. "You know he'd want you to find love again, have a family and live your life. That's what the dream was telling you. He was giving you his blessing." Nicholas eased her out of his embrace, took the handkerchief from his top pocket and dried her tears.

"Yes, I know." She gazed around. "You've done an amazing job of finishing the house, Nick. It's exactly as I envisioned it."

Nicholas took her hand and led her down the stairs. "I used the original plans. For you, Prue. I know you can be happy here."

She sighed. "I want to believe that."

He walked her into the living room and sat her in an armchair. "Then believe it, darling, because this is where you belong. It's your home."

She ran her eyes over the well-designed room then gazed up at him. "It's our home."

Nicholas took her in his arms and pressed his mouth to hers in a long kiss. When they parted, he looked into her eyes and said, "Let's go get married."

Prue nodded and smiled. "Yes, let's."

Forty eight

Their honeymoon destination was perfect. Prue sighed with happiness as she walked along the boardwalk hand in hand with her new husband and stepped inside the luxurious, over-water, double-story bungalow. A bottle of champagne and two glass flutes awaited them in the living room and upstairs their four post bed was adorned with palm leaves, apricot hibiscus flowers and white frangipani. Nicholas tipped the attendant, walked him out and thanked him before returning to his beautiful bride.

He wrapped his arms around her and breathed in the scent of her hair. "Like it?"

She slid her arms around his neck and smiled up at him. "I love it! Thank you, darling, it's amazing!"

Nicholas leaned in and planted a soft kiss on her lips. "You're welcome, Mrs. Colton."

Prue loved the sound of that. *Mrs. Colton.* Her smile widened. "It sounds so nice being called Mrs. Colton. I could get used to it."

"Well you'd better. We've got a long life ahead of us, you know." He smiled and kissed the tip of her nose. "Want some champagne?" He walked over to the lavish dark wood and glass coffee table, plucked the bottle from the ice bucket and loosened the cork without a pop. He poured two glasses, brought them out to their private patio and passed one to her. He raised his in a toast. "To a long and happy life together." She repeated his heartfelt declaration. It was all she could hope for. They clinked glasses and sipped the bubbly.

Prue gazed out at the crystal clear, azure water and spectacular view. "Just heavenly."

Nicholas came up behind her and slid an arm around her waist. "Yes, heavenly," he said, his tone seductive. He wasn't referring to their surroundings.

She turned around. "Why Mr. Colton are you flirting with me?" She reached across and sat her glass on the breakfast table. "What would my husband say?"

"It is your honeymoon, after all, Mrs. Colton. What could he say?" Nicholas winked, set his champagne flute down, held her face between his hands and pressed his lips to hers, their tongues entwined. He moved his mouth to the side of her throat and nuzzled her ear. "Want to go upstairs?"

Prue moaned with pleasure as he continued to nibble her ear and she unbuttoned his casual, blue and white checked shirt. "I thought you'd never ask."

Nicholas lifted her into his arms, wandered back through the living room, up the stairs and eased her onto the white bed cover. He shrugged out of his shirt and threw it into a chair, then pulled his board shorts off and tossed them across the room. He walked over, took hold of Prue's hands and pulled her to her feet.

Prue's heart thrummed as he spun her around and unzipped her cotton sun dress, slid the straps from her shoulders and allowed the floral garment to fall to the floor. She stepped out of it, turned to him and slid her arms around his neck, pressing her wanting lips to his. Nicholas threw the covers back, scooped her into his arms and laid her on the cool white sheets, then climbed over her and stared lovingly into her eyes. "I love you, Mrs. Colton."

Prue reached up and pulled him down onto her, wrapping her arms around him. "I love you, too, Mr. Colton."

He eased himself out of her embrace and stared into

her eyes for a long time. "You make me the happiest man alive, darling. I hope you know that."

Prue nodded and smiled, the love in her heart reflecting in her eyes. "Make love to me, Nick."

"With pleasure, my darling. Maybe we could try for a baby brother or sister for Nikki. What do you think?"

A playful smile spread across her face. "Sounds perfect."

They made love for the first time as husband and wife, cuddling and kissing in bed the whole afternoon. Prue couldn't have been happier. She gazed into Nicholas' loving eyes and ran her fingers through his dark hair. "I love making love with you. You're an incredible lover, you know that?"

"Why thank you, my darling. I'll always aim to please my beautiful wife. I adore making love to you too."

"Do you suppose we could do it again?" she asked, giving him a mischievous grin.

His eyes widened. "Again! Now?"

She nodded. "Well if we're going to make a baby brother or sister for Nikki we have to practice until we get it right, don't we?"

Nicholas grinned. "That's true. How about after dinner? I could muster up the energy for dessert."

"Mm, dessert sounds delicious. I can't wait." She pulled him close and kissed him long and hard.

After their one night together all those years ago it was extraordinary that they had found each other again. Had the tragedy of losing the love of their lives been the reason they had met that night? Had fate played a hand in bringing two broken hearts together? Prue believed anything was possible, how could she not after everything that had happened.

She was thankful to have the man she'd loved for so long in her life and grateful he was still in love with her. She was also grateful for the gift of their beautiful little girl. Her life was complete. They were a family at last and it was all Prue could ever have wished for.

www.ingramcontent.com/pod-product-compliance
Lightning Source LLC
Chambersburg PA
CBHW021953190626
46807CB00005BB/1933